"I don't want to live with you!"

Corrie was aghast. "I have a reputation to think about, you know."

Bryan arched an eyebrow and grinned. "Then you'd better not put ideas in my head."

"It's news to me that going out on one date leads to living together."

"That depends on the date. Let's just stick to admiring the leaves and forget about admiring each other."

If that wasn't a snub it was close enough to make Corrie's temper flare. "I don't know where you got the idea I was admiring you," she snapped.

"Your eyes said it. And in a way, you said it, too. You don't hint for a date with a man you don't like at least a little."

"As you said, that depends on the date."

Dear Reader:

The spirit of the Silhouette Romance Homecoming Celebration lives on as each month we bring you six books by continuing stars!

And we have a galaxy of stars planned for 1988. In the coming months, we're publishing romances by many of your favorite authors such as Annette Broadrick, Sondra Stanford and Brittany Young. Beginning in January, Debbie Macomber has written a trilogy designed to cure any midwinter blues. And that's not all—during the summer, Diana Palmer presents her most engaging heros and heroines in a trilogy that will be sure to capture your heart.

Your response to these authors and other authors of Silhouette Romances has served as a touchstone for us, and we're pleased to bring you more books with Silhouette's distinctive medley of charm, wit and—above all—romance.

I hope you enjoy this book and the many stories to come. Come home to romance—for always!

Sincerely,

Tara Hughes
Senior Editor
Silhouette Books

JOAN SMITH

Dear Corrie

Silhouette *Romance*

Published by Silhouette Books New York

America's Publisher of Contemporary Romance

SILHOUETTE BOOKS
300 E. 42nd St., New York, N.Y. 10017

ISBN: 0-373-08546-X

First Silhouette Books printing December 1987

America's Publisher of Contemporary Romance

Printed in the U.S.A.

Books by Joan Smith

Silhouette Romance

Next Year's Blonde #234
Caprice #255
From Now On #269
Chance of a Lifetime #288
Best of Enemies #302
Trouble in Paradise #315
Future Perfect #325
Tender Takeover #343
The Yielding Art #354
The Infamous Madam X #430
Where There's a Will #452
Dear Corrie #546

JOAN SMITH

has written many Regency romances, but likes working with the greater freedom of contemporaries. She also enjoys mysteries and Gothics, collects Japanese porcelain and is a passionate gardener. A native of Canada, she is the mother of three.

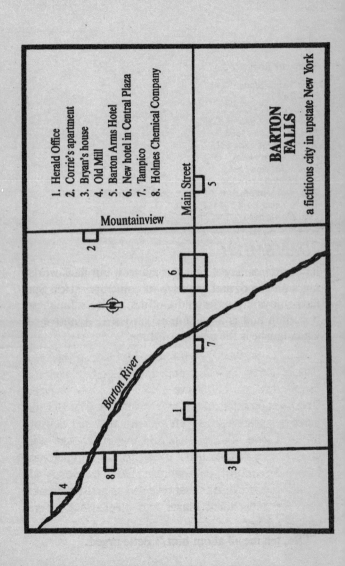

1. Herald Office
2. Corrie's apartment
3. Bryan's house
4. Old Mill
5. Barton Arms Hotel
6. New hotel in Central Plaza
7. Tampico
8. Holmes Chemical Company

Mountainview

Main Street

Barton River

BARTON FALLS

a fictitious city in upstate New York

Chapter One

As soon as Theo left, there was a tap at Corrie's apartment door and her neighbor peeked in. "Are you decent?" Bette called.

"No, you're among friends. Come on in," Corrie answered.

Bette Sanderson came in and lounged on the sofa beside Corrie. It was strange that these two women, different in just about every way, got along so well. Bette was an artist, older by nearly a decade. Her divorce two years ago had left her with an ironic view of life and love. Corrie wasn't just younger, she was conservative and idealistic. Even their appearance was in striking contrast. Bette wore her blond hair long and chose dramatic outfits that revealed an artistic streak. Corrie's understated blazer and pleated skirt were typical for her.

"So, tell me all about him," Bette urged.

"Not exactly awe-inspiring," Corrie admitted.

Bette lifted an elegantly arched brow in disbelief. "Dr. Manville a flop? I thought you'd really hit pay dirt this time—a doctor."

"He's a dentist, not an M.D."

"Still, free root canal work," Bette pointed out.

"Actually, he's an orthodontist. And I don't need root canal work, knock on wood. Theo says I have very nice teeth. Besides, I'm not going out with all these men for the freebies, you know."

"Yeah, I know—research. It's all part of the job," Bette said with a nod. As she examined her friend, she found it typical of fate that Corrie James had a whole string of dates subsidized by her boss, under the pretext of research.

With her looks, Corrie could get all the dates she wanted on her own. The artist in Bette appreciated the enviable luxuriance of Corrie's deep chestnut-colored hair. It swept back from her brow and waved around her chin. Those wide-set gray eyes lent a serious air that suited her. Most important of all, Corrie had good bones—a straight nose, firm jaw. Of course, Bette found her clothes dull but she admitted that her own raffish outfits wouldn't suit a rising newspaper journalist.

Bette drew her knees up under her flowing orange caftan, lifted her long blond hair over her shoulder and said, "Who's next on your list?"

"I'm seeing Theo again Saturday night."

"I thought you said he was a flop."

Corrie shrugged her shoulders. "He is, but he happens to desperately need a presentable date for Saturday. I let myself be talked into it."

"Softy!" Bette scoffed. Corrie needed a good talking to, and as Bette considered herself a sort of older sister, she was the one for the job. "You've got to learn how to say no. I never let men talk me into anything unless I want them to."

"Can *I* talk you into some coffee?"

"Sure, I wouldn't want to make the mistake of getting any sleep tonight. I'd probably dream of cuddly little kittens and balls of wool."

Corrie went to the kitchen. Her apartment was small enough that they could go on talking. "Still illustrating Kathy's Kittens, huh?"

"Yes, I've had them eat their porridge and clean their little teeth and put on their little dresses. Tomorrow I'll send them out to play in Kathy's garden. Did it ever occur to you, Corrie, that you and I both work in the field we chose, but not doing what we want to? I mean I didn't study fine arts for four years to end up painting kittens for children's books."

"I love my work!"

"You didn't have to study journalism to write columns on recipes and fashion," Bette pointed out.

"That's not all I do. I'm also the editor of the lifestyles section."

"The women's page," Bette interpreted.

"Men read it, too. I have my Saturday series on the interesting women of Barton Falls."

"It's the Kathy's Kittens of journalism, Corrie," Bette scoffed. "The trouble is, we're in highly competitive fields."

"You have to start somewhere. I'd rather do what I do than cover municipal meetings about new sewers or something. I'll make the coffee decaffeinated, okay?"

"Fine." Bette went to the kitchen and rooted through the cupboards for a snack. She put aside a box of whole wheat crackers and a bag of dried apricots. "Don't you have any junk food?"

"You are what you eat," Corrie warned, and opened the fridge.

"Oh Lord, am I turning into a potato chip?"

"Here, have an apple."

"*You* have an apple. It will keep Dr. Manville away. Why does he need this date Saturday? Is it a big party, or what? If it's an orthodontists' convention, I'm free to go with any dateless friend Doc might have."

Corrie rubbed the apple to make it shine and took a bite. "It's his high school reunion—cocktails, a dinner and dance. He wants to impress some woman—probably his old high school sweetheart. He doesn't want to go without a date anyway, and he doesn't seem to know any women."

"You'd think a dentist could get a date without using a dating service," Bette said. She gave a disconsolate look at the whole wheat crackers and took out two.

"Hey, dating services aren't just for the desperate, you know. Everybody's using them nowadays. They're a good way to meet people."

"Too bad they cost money," Bette said with a frown.

"What doesn't? I get dozens of letters at the paper inquiring about them. That's why I thought I should familiarize myself with how they work. Mr. Helmer agreed—the *Herald*'s footing the bill."

Bette gave her a knowing look. "Sure, sure. I don't suppose it has anything to do with the fact that your own office party is coming up, and you don't have a date?''

It was hard to fool Bette. Corrie gave a mental wince and poured the coffee. "That's just a coincidence. It's known as killing two birds with one stone."

"Also known as desperation tactics," Bette said, laughing. They returned to the sofa. "Aren't there any guys at the *Herald*?"

"Lots of them—all married, or involved, or so messed up you wouldn't want to go out with them."

"You must meet all kinds of other people through your work. Your business is people's life-styles. You must know how to meet men and get along with them. Your paper even has a psychologist on retainer for you to consult."

Corrie paused and set aside her apple. "Sure, I meet all kinds. I've interviewed men I'd love to know better, but a professional doesn't mix business and pleasure. Just the facts, ma'am. And the psychologist isn't my own personal matchmaker. I just consult with him when I'm covering some story with a psychological background. He helps me answer some of the letters I get."

"What's the most common problem you come across?" Bette asked.

Corrie didn't have to consider the answer for long. "I'd say it's an unwillingness to make a serious commitment. The world is full of playboys—and playgirls. It's not only the women that complain about that. I wonder why people are so afraid to commit themselves."

"Divorce is a hassle—an expensive hassle. Look at me," Bette pointed out. "I quit art school to put my ex through college. Now *he's* an engineer and I'm painting kittens to pay off my own college loan. I'd rather do it than take any money from Dave."

"You said 'no' once too often. He offered to pay you back," Corrie reminded her.

"The judge made him offer. I don't want anything from him except my freedom. Not that I didn't have plenty of that when we were married and he was playing musical beds. Speaking of bed, I'd better go. I have to be up bright and early to finish with Kathy's brood. Thanks for the coffee."

"They're not all like Dave," Corrie said gently. "See you tomorrow."

Bette left, and Corrie took the cups to the kitchen. Bette's problem was too often discussed to prey on her mind. She tidied her little apartment, smiling at the oasis of comfort she'd made for herself in the anonymous concrete block of apartments in Barton Falls. The city in upstate New York had seemed large to her after the small town in Maine where she'd grown up. Her apartment had seemed tiny, but it was all she could afford.

Too bourgeois, Bette had said when she saw it, but Corrie liked the traditional print sofa and mahogany coffee table. Her books and stereo equipment filled one wall. The framed prints above it had meaning to her—the brass rubbing she'd made at St. Alban's Church in England, the museum poster of Paul Klee's exhibition. The small oriental carpet was a parting gift from her parents and added a touch of class.

She straightened the magazines on the table and gave a last satisfied look. She wanted to get to bed early, too. This school reunion seemed to mean a lot to poor Theo. She hadn't told Bette the whole story. He wanted her to wear her sexiest dress and look glamorous to make someone called Georgie jealous. Georgie was apparently a lady it would be hard to make jealous.

Theo called Georgie "incredibly gorgeous." She was a model. Her family was rich and her brother apparently a genius. Just how Theo hoped to impress them with her poor self was a mystery, but she'd go whole hog and make a trip to the beauty parlor for him.

Corrie could sympathize with Theo. She only hoped she'd meet someone more attractive before the office party next month. Her ex, Harry Danton, would be there with his "incredibly gorgeous" new wife, Rhonda. Harry, the star football player turned sportswriter, had been positive he didn't want to make a commitment when she was going out with him. But when Rhonda came along, he had a diamond on her finger before you could say rice and old shoes. The pain was still sharp after two months. Would it never go away?

Was it her? Was there something the matter with her that Harry hadn't wanted to get married? "Let's have a trial run first," he had suggested. At least he hadn't used the phrase "shack up." Trial runs, she told him, were for cars, not people. Anger helped her through that rough time.

But it wasn't just her. The column she'd done on lack of commitment had brought in more letters than she usually got in a month. She was still answering them in her spare time. Her readers told her the problem was a new disease, endemic to her whole generation, both male and female. One day she'd find a man

who hadn't succumbed to the noncommitment infec-
tion. As the daughter of a minister, Corrie James had
been raised with high moral standards. "First marriage, then sex," her mother had said so often it had
become an integral part of Corrie's thinking.

She had discovered long ago that the morals of a
New England minister were different from other people's, but a New Englander never minded being a mi-
nority. And she was still a New Englander, even if she
had moved to Barton Falls. "When you find yourself
in the majority, it's time to reform," her father used
to say. He was an admirer of Ben Franklin's homey
wisdom.

"Perfectemundo! Great dress! It must have cost you
a bundle," Bette exclaimed when she stopped in to see
Corrie before her date the next night.

"It was on sale, but it still sent my credit card into
a state of shock," Corrie admitted.

"You look so beautiful I'd like to paint you."

"That's just rhetoric. You paint abstracts. What do
you really think? Is it too sexy?" Corrie asked uncertainly.

"My dear, you can't be too rich or too sexy."

Corrie went to the long mirror on the back of her
apartment door and examined herself. "I don't usually wear red," she said.

But maybe she would in future. It was flattering to
her dark coloring. The shimmering strands in the material highlighted her figure. The curve of her breast
seemed accentuated by the sharp nip in at the waist.
She wore her hair loose. The hairdresser had tousled
its smooth line, giving her an air of abandon. She

looked, she decided, like one of those people who had caught the noncommitment disease. She looked like a lady out for a good time and never mind tomorrow. Her father would hate it.

Bette looked with the artist's eye and said, "You can wear the primary colors. They overpower some people. Your dark hair and dark eyes balance them. Wear it to your own office party. You'll kill Harry in that getup," she added.

That was exactly the reason Corrie had bought it. She gave a mock innocent stare. "Harry? Oh, you mean Harry Danton."

"Yeah, Harry Danton, the hunk you were in love with last spring. You remember, the man that nearly made you give up your job so you wouldn't have to work near him when he jilted you."

"Oh, *that* Harry," Corrie said, and laughed to hide the pinching of her heart.

There was a tentative tap at the door. Corrie opened it to Dr. Theo Manville. While introductions were made, Bette stared at him and felt the red gown was going to be wasted. An older, pale-faced man with a slight paunch and glasses definitely wasn't worth it. He shyly handed Corrie a corsage.

Corrie looked with dismay at a cluster of pink baby roses. "How nice," she said, and smiled weakly.

Bette caught her eye and gave a grimace. "I'll put them on my coat," Corrie said.

Bette went to help her. "Lose them on the way, if at all possible," she whispered. Then she darted back to her apartment.

"You look perfect, Corrie," Theo said enthusiastically. "She'll be green with envy."

It wasn't very flattering to know he was only interested in making Georgie jealous, but Corrie didn't really mind. She was only going to this reunion to help Theo with his love life.

"If we happen to be talking to Georgie Holmes," he added nonchalantly, "I don't plan to tell her we just met. You don't mind?"

"You'd better tell me about our past relationship," she suggested.

"I haven't had time to work it out. I had a last-minute emergency. Bobby Thomson got a pin stuck in his braces. Just go along with whatever I tell her. You'll never see Georgie again, so I don't suppose it matters to you."

"No, it doesn't really matter to me," she said listlessly.

There was something radically wrong with her life when she had gone to the trouble and expense of this date for a man who didn't matter to her. Too softhearted, Bette would say, but she sympathized with Theo. Maybe if she was helpful to him, some benign deity would take pity on her and send her an incredible hunk to introduce to Harry. But that was wrong, too. Spiting an old flame shouldn't be her top priority.

Theo accompanied her to his car. He drove a conservative Ford that wouldn't impress a fashion model one bit. His dark and conservative suit wouldn't impress her, either. He had all the accoutrements of a middle-aged businessman. She was becoming curious to see this Georgie Holmes. What would Theo's idea of an incredibly gorgeous woman be? Probably some tight-lipped, prim little prude who modeled oxfords.

The reunion of Barton Falls High School was no grand or elegant affair. It was held at the old Barton Arms Hotel, and not the more chic new high-rise hotel in the redeveloped city center. There was a placard in the lobby welcoming the students of the past fifteen years. At a desk, they were given a self-adhesive name tag to stick on their clothes. It didn't stick very well to the metallic threads of Corrie's gown, but it made a good excuse to leave the pink corsage behind. No one else was wearing a corsage, she noticed. Theo took her possessively by the elbow and began to stroll through the throng attending the cocktail party.

He introduced her to half a dozen old classmates. She figured Theo must be a graduate of the oldest class there. That would put him somewhere in his early thirties, while some of the crowd were barely out of their teens. She met the expected mix of successful and nonsuccessful, and Theo told her a little about the people—the great football star who ended up clerking in a department store; the mousy girl who blossomed into a beauty and became a lawyer; the brain who owned his own software company.

But while he mentioned all this he kept looking around, obviously for Georgie Holmes. After two watery cocktails dinner was announced, and she still hadn't arrived. After the rubber chicken and chocolate mousse were eaten and five speeches delivered, there was still no Georgie. With luck, Theo might agree to leave before the dance.

"Let's just wait a little longer," he said, looking once more to the door. "She might drop in for the dance. Georgie loves to dance."

The throng moved along to the ballroom, where everyone waited in groups for the music to start. Corrie knew the minute Theo had spotted his quarry. He didn't just fall silent, he seemed to go into a coma. He stared at the doorway and gulped. Corrie followed the line of his gaze and could understand why.

Georgie really was incredibly gorgeous, and neither "prim" nor "prude" could be included in her description. The most surprising thing was her age. Georgie had to be a decade younger than Theo. She couldn't possibly be his high school sweetheart—she'd have been in kindergarten at that time.

The soft cloud of hair drifting around Georgie's shoulders looked like moonbeams. A heart-shaped face floated in the midst of it. Her large green eyes were heavily outlined with kohl, and she wore a dress that belonged in a fashion magazine. What there was of it was black; consisting mostly of straps, strategically placed to hide the important features of her anatomy.

Corrie recognized her face from the covers of fashion magazines. A path magically opened for her and her escort as they advanced into the room. Georgie nodded and smiled like a member of the royal family. No one was gauche enough to suggest she apply a name tag to her gown. Actually, there wasn't a strap wide enough to take it. She would have had to wear it on her hip.

As Georgie drew nearer, Corrie glanced to see who she was with. She half expected to see a movie star or television personality. She didn't recognize the man, but he certainly belonged on the wide screen. If a casting director had gone to Hollywood to select a date for her, he couldn't have done better. A fellow model, Corrie decided.

He was a head taller than Georgie, and Georgie wasn't short. She was tall and willowy enough to bring to mind the word anorexia. His hair wasn't quite as exotic a shade. It was tow-colored, lightened to gold on top, and he wore it slightly long, waved back from his brow. A pair of eyes, green like Georgie's, glowed in his tanned face. He spotted some friend and smiled, revealing a set of teeth that Theo would adore. Perfect for a toothpaste ad. He was the California boy type, suggesting sun and surfboards and romance. Under that jacket, Corrie was sure there was a perfect ripple of bronzed pectoral muscles. She felt a little warm just thinking of them.

Corrie felt a hand tighten on her elbow. "My God, she's seen me! She's coming!" Theo whispered. He sounded anguished.

Georgie was indeed coming toward them, with her date a step behind her. His broad shoulders were covered by the only white jacket in the room. Corrie noticed his ruffled shirtfront, then her eyes glided lower. Impeccably knife-creased black trousers and black patent leather loafers completed his outfit. When she raised her eyes, the vision was gazing at her. His lips curved in appreciation and his green eyes smiled. Men! They were all alike. Here he was with incredibly gorgeous Georgie and casting eyes at her. Maybe she could induce him to take her to the office party. Wouldn't he blow Harry Danton's socks off!

"Theo! Theo Manville! How nice to see you!" Georgie squealed. It was an unfortunate voice, young and squeaky, but it suited Georgie.

"Oh, it's Georgia Holmes, isn't it?" Theo asked, as though he wasn't quite sure he remembered her name.

"Look Bryan," Georgie said, and turned to speak to her date. So that was his name, Bryan. The next thing Corrie noticed was that Bryan had been waylaid by a striking redhead. The woman put her hand on his elbow and drew him into her group, where loud talk and laughter soon erupted.

Corrie pulled her attention back to her own group. She saw Georgie blink her green eyes in surprise. "Didn't you recognize me, Theo?" she asked. "I haven't changed that much, have I? Just my teeth straightened, and you did that. Theo's the best orthodontist in the state, isn't he, Miss...?" She looked to Theo for an introduction.

If Theo was the man responsible for this model's row of very straight pearly whites, he was certainly a lot older than Georgie.

"Miss James, Corrie James," Theo said. "And this is one of my ex-patients, Corrie—Georgia Holmes."

"Nice to meet you," Georgie said, shaking Corrie's hand. The girl looked so friendly that it was impossible not to like her. There was a vulnerable quality to her—half Victorian cameo, half siren.

"Ex-patient" was a strangely cold description of the woman Theo had been moaning over. He sounded as if Georgie were practically a stranger. Corrie realized that she was being subjected to a very close scrutiny. Georgie's green eyes raked her from head to toe, taking in every detail, yet there was no hostility in the smile she wore.

"I love your dress. Intense!" Georgie said admiringly.

So that was what she'd been assessing. "Thank you."

"Did Theo fix your teeth, too?" Georgie asked.

"Corrie's teeth are *naturally* straight," Theo said smugly. "Actually, we met in Acapulco last January."

Corrie frowned at this piece of fiction, but didn't want to deny it outright.

Georgie gave a bright smile and said, "I wish I'd known you were there, Theo. I was on a modeling assignment in Cancun. We might have arranged to get together."

Was Georgie incredibly subtle, or did she not realize Theo was trying his darnedest to make her jealous? Theo put an arm around Corrie's waist and pulled her against his hip. As he did so, Bryan broke away from the older group and joined them. "We were pretty busy," Theo said, smiling lovingly at Corrie.

"A convention, was it?" Georgie asked. "Are you a dentist too, Miss James?"

Before she could answer, Theo spoke up again. "Corrie a dentist?" he asked, and laughed. "Don't tell me you don't recognize Corrie James! She's a journalist. Corrie was on assignment, doing an article for a magazine. But then you don't read much, do you, Georgie?"

Georgie looked as guilty as a kitten with cream on its whiskers. It was Bryan who answered. "Georgie reads as much as she has time for. She's very busy."

Bryan's voice was a masculine rumble in his throat. There was a tinge of anger that Corrie could well understand. Why on earth was Theo acting like such an idiot and doing everything in his power to alienate the woman he'd come here to see?

"What magazine?" Georgie demanded.

Corrie didn't like to contradict Theo outright, but she wasn't going to abet him in this charade. She looked to Theo for the answer.

"*Time* magazine," he said.

"Wow! Fabulous!" Georgie beamed, and gazed at Corrie as though she were a genius.

Time was the only magazine Theo read, other than his trade publications. "The cover story—you might have seen the cover. Georgie is always looking at magazine covers, to see if she's on them," he added aside to Corrie in a disparaging way. She wanted to hit him, and the glint of anger in Bryan's eyes hinted that he shared her impulse.

Corrie had had a few free-lance articles accepted by women's magazines. That must be the grain from which this monumental lie had sprouted. Georgie appeared to swallow it, but Bryan, who now stood behind her, lifted an eyebrow and let his anger dwindle to amusement.

"So you work for *Time*!" Georgie exclaimed in wonder.

This had gone far enough. "No, I don't," Corrie said firmly.

"I said the article was free-lance," Theo inserted quickly. "Corrie works for a newspaper. You know these Vassar girls—so ambitious. She's also writing a novel."

Corrie had mentioned a hope of writing a novel some day. There was a latent grain of truth in that remark, but claiming she had attended prestigious Vassar College was another outright lie, pulled out of the air to impress Georgie. Corrie squirmed with embarrassment, especially as Bryan gave a sneering smile. She felt a rush of heat rise up the column of her neck and knew she was blushing.

"My mother went to Vassar," Georgie mentioned. "The men got all the brains in my generation."

"You can see who got the looks," Bryan said, smiling encouragement at Georgie, who smiled back.

"Georgia flunked out of secretarial school," Theo added, quite unnecessarily.

"Georgie gave up secretarial school when she got a very lucrative offer from a modeling agency," Bryan corrected.

"Oh, you're a model!" Corrie said, hoping to smooth over the ruffled waters. "That must be very interesting."

"Yes, my next assignment out of the country is modeling fur coats in Quebec. They shoot the pictures months in advance. Quebec's in Canada."

And still Bryan went on staring at Corrie, assessing her in a way that said very clearly he despised her. Of course he suspected Theo was lying his head off, but that look suggested Corrie was the originator of the lies. There was a glint of anger in the green eyes that studied her so closely that she felt like a blot on a microscope plate. His lips were held in a tight line, and his nostrils quivered in disgust. In spite of his angry expression, he was still the most beautiful man Corrie had ever seen. She could feel an electrical pull coming from his rigid body. Who was he? Why didn't Georgie introduce him?

Theo didn't leave much time for introductions. He was off on another wildly unbelievable story. "Canada!" he exclaimed. "That's a coincidence. Corrie's family owns a mine in Quebec. They live there. We were thinking of taking a quick trip up ourselves—if Corrie can get away, that is. She's very busy."

Bryan gave a sneering look. "Dashing off to Stockholm to accept a Nobel prize?" he asked.

"Vassar, her alma mater, wants her to do a series of guest lectures actually," Theo said.

The music began, and Theo said, "They're playing our song, darling. Let's dance. Nice talking to you, Georgia."

Corrie was glad to escape and took the opportunity to scold Theo. "What's the matter with you? You couldn't have done a better job of turning Georgie off if you'd beaten her with a club!"

"I was just trying to make her jealous," he said. "I think it's working."

"You can use some other poor unfortunate to make her jealous. I felt like an idiot." Over Theo's shoulder, she saw Bryan and Georgie begin to dance. They made a stunning couple. Both moved with easy grace, while poor Theo looked like a raccoon suffering some strange sort of convulsion.

"It's only for one night," Theo pointed out. "What do you care what she thinks of you? You'll never see her again."

"I hope not!"

It was, of course, not Georgie's opinion she cared about. Though she probably wouldn't ever see Bryan again, either, so maybe it didn't matter. But it had been damned embarrassing.

"Is Bryan a model, too?" she asked.

Theo looked at her as though she were insane. "Oh, no. He runs the Holmes plant. They make medicine—antibiotics and things."

"I know," Corrie said. "The chemical plant. Is Georgie one of *the* Holmeses?"

You couldn't live long in Barton Falls and not know the name Holmes. They were one of the founding families and still one of the largest employers. There was the old Holmes building on the main street, and Holmes park, the new industrial plant. If Bryan ran the plant, it seemed a pretty good bet he was a white-haired boy with the Holmes family. They'd love the idea of Georgie marrying him. Theo had about as much chance as a snowball in a microwave oven, though Georgie did seem to like him.

"I thought he was probably some model Georgie met at her work," she said.

"About Quebec," Theo said pensively. "I've got to find out exactly when she's going. Maybe you and I could—"

"Forget it, Theo," Corrie said firmly. "This is the only chance you'll have to use *me* to lure Georgie back."

Now why did that make him smile moonishly? She followed Theo's gaze and saw him looking at Georgie. Georgie lifted her hand and waggled her fingers, still smiling.

"I'm going to ask her for the next dance," he said. "You'll have to dance with Bryan. You don't mind?"

Bryan turned his head to see who Georgie was waving to. He met Corrie's look and gazed at her long enough to show some interest.

An impish smile curved Corrie's lips. "Well, since it's for a good cause," she said.

"Thanks. You're a good kid."

Chapter Two

The orchestra struck up a romantic ballad. "Just like old times," Georgie said as she went into Theo's arms.

Corrie stood beside Bryan, waiting for him to ask her to dance. She felt a moment of awful disappointment when Bryan's gaze wandered around the room, obviously looking for a different partner. Whatever made her think he'd dance with her? He'd made his aversion plain enough. He was probably a Barton Falls High grad too. There must be dozens of girls here he'd like to dance with.

To let him off the hook, Corrie said, "I'll just go and powder my nose."

Bryan studied her nose in the shadowed light of the ballroom. A very cute nose the girl had, but he didn't much care for her habit of carrying it in the air. "It doesn't look shiny to me," he said.

"It's known as an euphemism."

Spunky. Lord, how tired he was of spunky women. But she was really very pretty. That red dress—he'd spotted it the minute he'd come into the room. It clung in all the right places, to all the right curves. "Hurry back. We don't want to miss the whole dance," he said.

"Oh, well, in that case, I won't bother powdering my nose."

Bryan scanned her face from his superior height. He hadn't realized she was so short until they stood head to shoulder. The top of her head would just about brush his chin—the right height for dancing. And she was a good dancer, he'd noticed.

"Euphemism is the wrong term," he corrected. "Fancy a *Time* stringer making a mistake like that." He drew her into his arms. "What it was was an excuse. It was either an attempt to escape dancing with me or a polite way of letting me escape dancing with you. As your nose no longer needs powder, I'll assume it was the latter."

Corrie leaned her head back and smiled nervously. "Brilliant deducing." The words came out rather garbled. It was that zinger about the *Time* stringer that unnerved her. It was a challenge, and one she had no intention of taking up.

This wasn't her battle. She'd try to tread a thin line between not making a complete jackass of Theo and not confirming all his lies. It wasn't going to be easy. Strange how differently she looked at Bryan now that she knew he wasn't just a handsome physical specimen. His eyes, somewhere between the pale transparency of peridots and the deeper green of emeralds, no longer looked just sexy. She saw the intelligence lurking in their depths. The sexiness was still there but at the moment it took second place to the other.

Bryan studied her as she examined him. Now what had made her so edgy all of a sudden? He'd give her a little jab and see what happened. "It's strange Fred Helmer never mentioned that one of his journalists had done a cover story for *Time*. How long ago was that?" he asked, and read her guilty reaction.

The man certainly didn't believe in beating around the bush. Corrie gulped. "You know Mr. Helmer?" Oh Lord, her boss! If Bryan mentioned this load of rubbish to him ...

"We're old friends," Bryan replied. "And you didn't answer my question."

She cleared her throat, trying to find a path through this maze of deceit. "Theo got a little carried away. It wasn't a cover story actually."

"I didn't think so. It's hard to believe a writer of that caliber would be wasting her time describing the humdrum life-style of Barton Falls. Or are you syndicated, Dear Corrie?" he asked. There was an insinuating tone to his question. He knew all about her! He knew exactly what she did at the *Herald*.

No endearment was intended by the "Dear." "Dear Corrie" was the title of her weekly letter column. Readers wrote in with questions, which she tried to answer. A small photograph was included at the top of the column. Bryan must have recognized her. He used a derisive accent, and his tone put her on the defensive immediately.

"No, I'm not syndicated—yet! But describing the life-style of Barton Falls and advising readers is a worthwhile job."

A muscle at the edge of Bryan's lips quivered in angry distaste. "I have a piece of advice you can pass along to one lovelorn gentleman, specifically Dr. Manville. I don't want him pestering Georgie."

His very tone was an insult. Corrie held in the urge to lash out at him. Instead she smiled demurely. "I don't give unsolicited advice. I always find that so underbred, don't you?"

"Quite frankly, I find the whole idea of a girl your age setting herself up as an authority on anything more important than face cream ridiculous."

His dismissing tone was like adding oil to a fire. "That's why Mr. Helmer keeps a psychologist and a psychiatrist on retainer. If the column involves important interpersonal matters, they advise me. I put their advice into layman's terms. And I'm not a girl. I'm twenty-four years old."

He would have thought more like twenty-one. There was an air of uncertainty about Corrie that made her appear younger. "How many years out of Vassar?" he demanded.

Apparently he believed that lie. "I graduated three years ago," she replied, carefully omitting the word Vassar. "Is there anything else you'd like to know, Mr.—" It came as a surprise to Corrie that she didn't even know his last name.

"Call me Bryan. Yes, one more question. I'd like to know what your relationship to Theo is."

His arrogant way of demanding set her hackles up. Just who the hell did he think he was to be raking her over the coals? She gave him a bold look. "I should think that's quite obvious."

"It isn't. Humor me."

Corrie ignored the question that had become a command. "Lovely party. Are you a graduate of Barton Falls High, Bryan, or did you just accompany Georgie to the party?"

A grudging smile parted his lips, and a flash of white teeth showed in the shadows. "All right, so I'm overly protective. Georgia's just a kid, and Theo's—" He came to a stop.

"A what? Orthodontist? Nothing wrong with that."

"A thirty-three-year-old orthodontist. He was two years ahead of me in high school. He's too bloody old for Georgie, and too fast."

"Fast?" she asked, blinking in surprise.

"I don't mean he's a lecher. At least he didn't try to fly Georgia off to Mexico or Canada."

Corrie ground her teeth in futility. "So what was the problem?"

"He was trying to rush her into marriage when they'd only been dating for a month. She's eighteen years old, for God's sake. She doesn't know what she wants yet. Actually, I should be grateful he's found you, except that it hasn't seemed to quell his ardor for Georgie."

They both looked across the room to where Theo had Georgie in a firm bear hug as he pulled her around the floor. It would be hard to say which of them looked more blissful. He was probably telling Georgie the whole truth by now, that all the marvelous stories about herself were a load of manure. Corrie scowled.

"That hurts, does it?" Bryan taunted. "Don't tell me you've really fallen for him. I thought you were probably after free braces."

Bette had expressed a similar idea, but coming from Bryan it seemed more offensive. "Contrary to the popular opinion, women do date orthodontists for other reasons. My teeth are not crooked and neither are my morals."

Bryan inclined his head. His cheek brushed hers, and his lips hovered at her left ear. "I noticed, about the teeth I mean. About the morals, time will tell. Personally, I never let a little lack of morals come between . . . friends?"

A nervous flutter invaded her lungs at his touch and the intimacy of his breath in her ear. She was acutely aware of his arms around her, the lean, hard length of his body pressing hers. When had he tightened his grip? He wasn't holding her that way before. His thigh brushed hers as they moved to the music, and the flutter escalated to a quiver. It moved lower, into her abdomen.

It all happened before she even had time to digest his words. He was intimating the idea that he'd like to see her again. No doubt a little lack of morals in his female friends would suit him just fine. It was probably de rigueur.

She lifted her head back and stared at him. Her expression was rigid with disapproval. "Friends?" she asked. "I hardly know you."

"That's easily taken care of. Why don't we get rid of Theo and Georgie and go somewhere?" He waited impatiently to see how she reacted to this. A twenty-four-year-old woman was old enough to know the score. Apparently she was in the habit of traveling with Theo.

"To see your etchings, perhaps?"

"I see you're familiar with the game. But etchings are so common. I prefer originals like you, Corrie." The seductive purr in her ear sent goose bumps down her spine.

"Unfortunately, *I* prefer *gentlemen*," she said coolly.

"That is unfortunate!" he said, laughing lightly.

Corrie pulled away from him and left him standing alone in the middle of the floor looking like a fool. So he'd misread her. She wasn't going to be easy. That made the game more interesting. A tight grin played about his lips. Fortunately Corrie didn't see it as she paced swiftly toward the door. Bryan followed, stiff-legged and determined.

"Not an art lover?" he asked lightly, pretending not to be angry. "I also have a well-stocked wine cellar. Plenty of good reading material. *Newsweek*, *Time*..." he added satirically.

"*Playboy*?" she asked, and watched while his angry parody of a smile stretched to a grin.

"And *Playboy*," he agreed. "We all read it for the editorials, but a famous journalist like you would know that, Dear Corrie."

He was making fun of her, taunting her, and she'd had enough. "All right, so he exaggerated," she said, loud and clear. "I'm not a famous journalist. I write an unsyndicated life-style column for a small-city newspaper. Hemingway wrote for a newspaper too, you know. And lots of writers worked for customs and... Oh, never mind. He was just trying to impress—" Corrie came to a conscious stop. "His old school friends," she continued. "I didn't know he was going to turn into Walter Mitty on me."

"I think you mean Pinocchio."

"I mean Walter Mitty. Don't you recognize a fantasy when you hear one? That's what Theo wishes his life was like."

"It's hard to feel sorry for the best orthodontist in the state. He could afford to live out his fantasies."

Corrie frowned at this news. "Theo famous? I never heard of him before."

"Before what?" he asked swiftly. His mobile face was alert with the scent of something amiss.

"Before I met him," she said vaguely.

"And when was that?"

She gave him a cool look. "Recently."

"The reason you hadn't heard of him would be because you don't need braces. Believe me, Georgie wouldn't have anything but the best. Theo gets clients coming all the way from New York City."

Corrie scowled. "If I'd known that, I would have—" The truth nearly slipped out again. She wasn't used to living a lie, and she wasn't used to dealing with someone like Bryan. No man had ever looked at her with quite such a blatantly marauding pair of eyes. She almost blushed at what those green glittering gems suggested as they examined her.

She hurried on toward the lobby. The light was brighter here. Bryan was happy to see that Corrie looked as good in bright lights as in the semidarkness. He was surprised to see her eyes were gray; they had looked brown. Gray, he decided, was much more interesting. Those eyes gave her a serious but cool look.

"You wouldn't have come with him?" he asked. "What have you got against successful men?"

"We're only discussing one man, not a whole category."

"Good. I was afraid I might get included in your wrath." Bryan watched as her eyes clouded over and wondered what had got her dander up now.

What bothered Corrie was that this man she had no trouble disliking in the dark had just smiled in the light, revealing a new side of his personality. There was a boyish charm in him that she hadn't noticed before. The smile lurking at the back of his eyes wasn't just marauding; it held amusement, too.

"I don't know you well enough to dislike you."

"Yet," he added, and laughed. "We'll have to do something about that, Corrie."

She went toward the coat check booth and gave the attendant her ticket. She'd only come here so that Theo could make up with Georgie, and he had. She didn't have to stay and spar with this impossible man. Let him fight with Theo instead.

The corsage on her coat had turned brown around the edges. Bryan looked at it and shook his head. "A man who indulges in fantasies should have given an orchid. Theo's dreams, I fear, involve a rose-covered cottage and a picket fence."

"How depraved of him, actually planning to commit matrimony!" she snipped.

Bryan laughed lightly as he held her coat. "I've revealed myself! How did you plan to get home?" he asked.

"In a taxi. Would you mind telling Theo I left?"

Bryan hesitated a moment and said, "I'll drive you."

"You can't leave Georgie here alone."

"She won't be alone. She'll be with Theo." He apparently remembered that this wasn't what he wanted. "Wait a sec. I'll be right back." He hastened toward the ballroom at a purposeful stride. Even from the rear Bryan looked like a man who meant business.

Within seconds he was back with Theo and Georgie in tow. "I'm sorry you have a headache, Corrie," Georgie said.

"And she isn't even home yet," Bryan threw in with a laughing look.

Georgie shook her head at him. "Bryan!"

So that was the excuse Bryan had come up with. Hardly original, but he had managed to turn even that into something suggestive. "It'll be fine once I get home. It's just the noise," she said, aiming her explanation at Georgie. It struck her as strange that Georgie should be the most reasonable and most likable of the three.

Theo turned to Georgie and said, with no particular attempt at secrecy, "I'll be back in half an hour."

Bryan, standing behind Theo, lifted his eyebrows and smiled. Corrie gave him a look that would freeze fire. "Good night, folks. Nice to have met you," she said grimly.

Theo began complaining as soon as they were out the door. "I don't see why we have to leave so soon. It was going great with Georgie."

"Well, it wasn't going great with Bryan! Why did you make up those stupid lies about me? *Time* magazine, for heaven's sake. And Bryan knows my editor."

Theo attempted a menacing growl, which sounded remarkably like a kitten's mewl. "Bryan—it's all his fault. He's the one that broke us up."

"I wish you luck, Theo, but frankly, I think you've got pretty stiff competition. The family must approve of him if he runs their company."

They reached the car, and Theo unlocked her door. "What? What do you mean?"

"You said Bryan runs the Holmes plant, didn't you?"

"Well, of course he runs it. He owns the bloody thing now that their father's dead."

Corrie slid onto the seat in a state of bewilderment, and Theo slammed the door. By the time he got in the other side, she had made sense of his words. "*Their* father?" she demanded.

"Yes, old Jerome Holmes. He was Bryan and Georgie's father."

"You mean they're brother and sister?" Her voice came out in a squeak.

"Of course. I told you that."

"You did not!"

"You must have seen the family resemblance. They look alike, except that on her it looks good. It doesn't matter anyway. Georgie's moving to New York. It's too much of a hassle commuting to the city for her assignments, so she's leaving home. I have a lot of clients from the city," he added pensively.

Corrie could almost hear the gears grinding as he figured out his future. He and Georgie in New York, away from Bryan's influence.

"Bryan thinks she's too young to settle down."

"He wouldn't think so if she weren't his sister. Yes, he would, though. He doesn't approve of marriage. That guy has a lot of nerve putting me down, the way he plays around. At least I want to marry her."

A red light flashed in Corrie's head. "I got the idea he was a playboy," she said, and listened with avid interest for any details Theo might provide.

"Oh yeah, a macho man. Love 'em and leave 'em— that's his motto."

"That's what I thought. I wonder why he wore such a fancy outfit to the school reunion. No one else did."

"They had been at a party in New York. That's why they were so late. Georgie made him take her to the reunion, hoping I'd be there."

"Well, I'm glad you're getting your chance with Georgie, Theo," she said. As for the reason for Georgie wanting to go to the dance, it was more fantasy on his part.

"We're invited to her party next Saturday."

Corrie gave a jerk. "We?"

"Bryan's having a going away party for her next Saturday before she leaves for New York. You've got to go with me, Corrie. She asked you, too. She thinks we're going steady."

It was too ludicrous. Corrie put her head back on the seat and laughed out loud. "Theo, you're never going to get any place with her if she thinks you're serious about me."

"You don't know Georgie like I do," he smiled contentedly. "She's like her brother. They always had everything they wanted, so what they want now is what they think they can't have. It's from being born rich." This simplistic explanation seemed to satisfy him completely.

Corrie thought of Bryan as she pondered his explanation. It made a peculiar sort of sense, and it explained Bryan's passing interest in herself. She hadn't fallen for him—well, she hadn't let him see it, anyway.

Maybe if she could hold him at arm's length until the office party, she could invite him. He'd be the perfect escort to show Harry Danton how little she missed him. But the party was a month away. According to Theo, Bryan's amours lasted only until he had succeeded. A month was a long time to keep a man like that at bay.

"Will you go with me next Saturday?" he asked. "Please, Corrie. You can't let me down."

Corrie thought a minute before giving her answer. Maybe it was worth a try. Harry Danton could say goodbye to his socks if she went to the party with Bryan.

"All right, Theo, but only under certain conditions. Don't tell any more fantastic lies about me, or us. You practically announced we were lovers with that stupid Mexico story." Was that why Bryan was interested in her? She'd sounded like an easy conquest.

"I don't have to say any more. She's got the idea now," Theo said contentedly.

"So has her brother."

"Don't worry. You're not his type," Theo assured her. "And I mean that as a compliment."

The Harry Danton problem had taken on a different coloring when Corrie went to bed that night. The feeling of lonely desperation she had come to consider a permanent part of her life was gone. Her pride still demanded that she show up at the Christmas party with an exquisite man, and she knew she wouldn't find one who filled the bill better than Bryan Holmes. But this was now only a childish desire to look good in

front of an old boyfriend. The deep hurt had sub-
sided. It was easy to forget it and concentrate on the
more interesting problem.

The problem was of a man who activated every
hormone in her body and probably knew it. A man
who didn't believe in marriage and thought she was of
the same opinion. A man she intended to lead on just
enough to drag him to that party in a month's time. At
least Bryan would be easier to forget after it was over.
All she had to do was make sure she didn't go and fall
in love with him.

Fat chance. Once bitten, twice shy. This time she
knew what she was doing. She wouldn't make the
mistake of thinking he was serious or of becoming serious herself.

Chapter Three

"Dear Corrie," the letter began. "I couldn't agree more with what you wrote in your column on lack of commitment. I'm in love with a terrific guy and would like to make it permanent." Corrie hardly had to finish the rest of it. She'd come to recognize the pattern. Sure enough, the terrific guy was kind, loving and fun, and not at all interested in a serious commitment. The mail was still coming in from that column. It deserved a follow-up, except that nothing had changed. There was nothing new to say on the matter, but she'd write a personal reply anyway.

Her answer wasn't what the writer really wanted to hear. "If you want to settle down with one man forever, and the terrific guy wants to be footloose, give him an ultimatum. If he opts out of the relationship, don't despair. There's more than one perfect mate out there. Forget him, get busy and find one who feels as you do."

Corrie felt dissatisfied as she folded up the answer and put it in the envelope. It was easy to write "forget him," but it was hard to do. She found it increasingly hard to forget Bryan Holmes, and she'd only met him once. She thought he'd call before now. At least it was Friday. One week of the four preceding the office party had passed without having to worry about keeping Bryan at bay. She'd see him tomorrow night at Georgie's going away party.

Saturday Corrie left work at noon. After a quick cleanup of the apartment, she went shopping with Bette. When they finished, they stopped at Bette's apartment for coffee.

"So tonight's the big do, huh?" Bette said. "How come you aren't getting your hair done?"

"I didn't have time."

Bette handed her a tollhouse cookie containing approximately five hundred calories. "I'll do it up for you, if you like."

Bette's artistic flair went beyond painting. Her apartment, other than the studio room, which was rather a mess, was a dazzling success. She was a wizard with hair and makeup, too. Corrie looked around at the off-white walls decorated with samples of Bette's more serious painting. She really was good. It didn't seem possible that the woman who painted those cute kittens in frilly dresses had done the severe modern abstracts in the room.

"Would you?"

"My pleasure," Bette mumbled through a mouthful of cookie. "If you were smart, you'd try to nab

Theo. I had no idea he was so prominent. My editor from New York's been bragging for years about the wonderful orthodontist she sends her kids to, and it turns out he's Theo. You've hit the mother lode, Corrie. Go for it.''

"He's in love with Georgie Holmes."

"That model with the funny hair? A kitten," Bette said dismissingly. "She doesn't have your bone structure. She'll look like nothing when she's fifty."

"Meanwhile she looks like a million bucks. Besides, Theo's not my type."

Bette looked unconvinced. "He's the type who wants to get married. That kind of a guy is practically extinct, Corrie. I wish I was the one who was going out with him."

Corrie gave her an encouraging smile. "Georgie's leaving town. Why don't you come over to my place for a drink before we leave tonight?"

Bette considered it, then said, "Nah. If he likes kittens, he wouldn't like an old cat like me."

"You're not old. You're younger than he is. Oh gosh, look at the time."

"How old is he?" Bette asked, examining her cookie.

"Thirty-three."

"Hmm."

"I'd better go. He's picking me up at eight. Feel free to come over if you change your mind."

Corrie dashed into her apartment and put away her groceries. She made a chicken sandwich and heated a bowl of soup before starting her preparations. As she showered, her mind roamed over what Bette had said. Funny how dull old Theo yearned for a young girl like

Georgie. What did he see in her outside of a pretty face? And what had she seen in Harry Danton? He was a handsome jock, but for the most part it had just been chemistry. It was probably a good thing he hadn't asked her to marry him.

Everyone at the office knew she'd been jilted, so it wasn't just Harry she wanted to avenge herself on. She still wanted to march into that office party with a handsome hunk on her arm, and she hadn't met many hunks as handsome as Bryan Holmes. So tonight she'd have Bette do up her hair, she'd wear her sexiest dress and flirt a little with him.

Black was the color of seduction, but unfortunately black didn't do a thing for her chestnut hair. Bryan had already seen her red dress, so she'd wear her cream jersey. It clung like a second skin and dipped low in the back. She brushed a frosting of silver shadow on her eyelids and added a touch of lipstick. After she had on her makeup, Corrie went to check the effect in a full-length mirror.

She smoothed the jersey material over her waist and hips. It would feel soft and sensuous if Bryan . . . She glanced at her face in the mirror, noticing the excitement sparkling in her eyes and the stain of pink flushing her cheeks. Dope! She shook the thought away and went to call Bette to do her hair.

She noticed Bette had done her own hair and face as well. She wore an artistic floating cloud of peacock blue over a pair of black satin slacks and looked fabulous. Bette gave a disparaging shrug.

"I thought I might just stick around when Theo comes to call," she said. "No harm in trying. Hey, that dress looks terrific. You must have some serious seduction in mind."

"No, nonserious, but it requires the same effort. Make me beautiful if you can."

"That shouldn't be too much trouble," Bette said, and led Corrie to the vanity.

With a few flicks of the brush and a couple of hairpins, Bette performed her magic. A tousled pile of chestnut curls perched precariously atop Corrie's head, with tantalizing tendrils playing around her ears.

"You don't want to look too neat," Bette said, flicking a curl. "If you bind your hair up too tightly, it suggests men shouldn't touch it. This do is an invitation."

On this piece of advice, the door buzzer sounded. Corrie looked at her friend in the mirror and said, "Why don't you get it, Bette? I'll give you a few minutes."

Within one minute, she heard the sound of relaxed laughter coming from the living room. Now why couldn't Theo be sensible and fall for someone like Bette? She was a nice person. A good, thoughtful friend who wanted to get married and settle down. Here Theo was thinking of uprooting his business to New York.... All for an eighteen-year-old kid who, Corrie concluded, only gave him the time of day because she felt sorry for him.

Corrie waited a few minutes before joining them. "Sorry I'm late," she said, glancing to Bette, who winked broadly.

"That's all right," Theo smiled. "Bette was just telling me about her work. It sounds interesting."

"I didn't know you were interested in—"

"About my oil painting," Bette said quickly. This was to let Corrie know she didn't want to talk about her book illustrations. "Theo's interested in art. He's going to look at my work sometime. He wants a painting for his waiting room. What a chance for me! So many people would see it there." Bette gave an admiring smile.

Theo blushed with modest pride. "I do seem to draw a lot of well-heeled people," he admitted.

"They're the only kind that can afford your prices," Bette said, laughing. "I'd love to get my teeth straightened, but the cost!"

Theo lowered his head and stared at her teeth. "It wouldn't take much. It's only the two front teeth that are slightly overlapped at the bottom. Your roots aren't crowded. A retainer would do it."

"How much would it cost?" Bette asked.

"Maybe we can arrange some barter," Theo suggested. "I'll drop in and see your paintings the next time I'm calling for Corrie. We're in a bit of a hurry now."

"What next time?" Corrie asked sharply.

For no discernible reason Theo laughed. Corrie suggested they all have a drink, but Theo was anxious to leave.

They left Bette at her door and went to the car. Theo drove toward the western side of town, to the old established residential neighborhood where large lawns and gardens lent an air of luxury. The size and grandeur of the houses increased as they drove. Old-fashioned black iron lamps beamed on mature trees, giving a hint of their beautiful autumn colors. Corrie tried not to be impressed when he drove up in front of a stone mansion with a fanlight and pillars. She didn't have to ask if this was the Holmes house. The cars parked in front told her there was a party going on.

She felt uncertain and inadequate when a servant answered the door. Lord, Bryan must be a million-aire, she thought. She'd probably be the only woman there without a fur coat. A vast marble entranceway stretched before them. The sound of raucous rock music pounded from the distance. That didn't sound too pompous anyway.

Before any more doubts had time to form, Bryan came along the hallway toward them. He wore a navy cashmere sweater and jeans. Corrie gave a horrified look at Theo and felt a strong wish that the floor could open and swallow her. She should have known a teen-ager wouldn't be having a stately, formal party.

Bryan's green eyes blinked in surprise as he got close enough to see her hairdo and the front of her slinky dress.

"Good evening," he said, nodding to them both. "Come on in. The bash is in full swing. Maybe you'd like to put your coat upstairs, Corrie?"

"Yes, thanks."

She darted up the curving staircase, holding her coat to hide her dress. She sat on the bed and moaned. There were a few denim jackets tossed casually on the bed, one wild plaid blanket coat and a leather jacket. She didn't bother looking around for furs. She knew she'd come in the wrong style. What she didn't know was what she could do about it, short of going home to change.

At least she could let her hair down. She took off her coat and went to the mirror. She matched the room if not the party. It was a lovely room, large and furnished with mahogany antiques. With the brush in her hand, she stood thinking. Changing her hair wouldn't make much difference. She'd still have on a fancy dress and spike-heeled sandals. Georgie and Bryan had been overdressed at the high school reunion, and they hadn't seemed to mind.

She stuck the brush back in her purse and went downstairs. Bryan and Theo stood at the bottom of the stairs, waiting for her. Theo was looking around for Georgie. It was Bryan who turned toward her as she descended.

The lamp overhead gilded his hair and cast a bronze light on his rugged face. Beneath his sweater she saw the breadth of wide shoulders, firm chest and board-flat stomach. The outline of his strong thighs was visible beneath the tight jeans. Bryan finished his own examination, and their eyes met.

She felt weak at the impact of those green eyes devouring her. She read all sorts of messages in them. To break the mood she said, "I'm afraid I'm overdressed."

"Theo told me you'd been to New York for dinner," he replied. A glint of white teeth flashed in a smile. He added in a low aside, "Keep up the good work, Corrie. Tomorrow Georgie will be gone to New York, and you and I can start becoming friends."

So that was why he hadn't called! He wanted her to keep Theo tied up till Georgie was safely away from the danger of marriage. It didn't occur to her for another few seconds that Theo was doing it again—telling lies to impress the Holmes family. She wondered just where they were supposed to have dined. She gave

Theo an accusing stare. He straightened his tie and said, "Shall we join the party, darling?"

While she grimaced at the casual endearment, he took her hand and led her away. Bryan stood at the bottom of the stairs, looking after them. The view, he found, was admirable. That clinging dress really accentuated Corrie's body. He smiled in anticipation and walked after them.

Theo drew to a stop at the doorway and began searching for Georgie. She wasn't hard to spot. The white minidress with black polka dots roughly the size of oranges stood out, even in the midst of the other outlandish costumes. Her long hair was pulled into a ponytail that started at the top of her head and flew when she danced. Corrie winced at the deafening music and looked around at the dancers. There was a lot of orange hair being worn that fall. Also a lot of purple sweaters, the long, loose kind that came to slightly above the knees. Georgie's guests were just kids. Surely Theo could see how out of place he was amidst this set.

He smiled foolishly and grabbed Corrie's hand. "Let's boogie," he said.

The next fifteen minutes rated as some of the longest and most uncomfortable of Corrie James's life. She was bounced and pushed around the floor by Theo, who looked like nothing so much as an elephant at a high school hop. His sedate gray suit and white shirt stuck out a mile and were as out of place as his efforts at dancing. One writhing teenager said, "Sorry, sir," when he bumped into him.

"No sweat, man," Theo called back.

At last the hideous dancing was over and Corrie headed for the farthest, darkest corner. "Theo, this is ridiculous," she panted. "We look like a couple of senior citizens at a pep rally. I think we should cut out—now."

Theo wiped his brow and looked around for some chairs. "The party's a little rowdier than I thought," he admitted. "I never met any of Georgie's friends before. When I was out with her, we went to a play, and twice to dinner—just the two of us. She seemed...different," he said, frowning.

"Well, now you've seen what she's really like. Young, Theo. She's young."

Gazing across the room, he said wistfully, "This isn't the real Georgie. It's only an act she puts on, to cover her lonesomeness. She's really sensitive and shy. She writes poetry," he added, as though that proved it.

"I think the 'sensitive and shy' bit was probably the act," Corrie suggested doubtfully.

"She likes older men. Some women do. It can make a good marriage."

There was obviously no point in trying to have a serious talk at this public place, but Corrie decided she'd talk it over with the psychologist her paper kept on retainer and see if she could find some good advice for Theo. Meanwhile, there was an awful night to be endured, although with luck she'd have another chance to talk to Bryan.

She looked around the room, but he wasn't there. Wise man! He knew enough to stay away from this teenage party. Georgie looked around, and when she spotted Theo, she started walking toward him.

"Hi, Theo. Glad you could come," she smiled politely. "Corrie, intense!" she added, looking at her hair and dress. "Jersey's so personal, isn't it?"

It was just as well Georgie didn't wait for an answer. Corrie didn't know what possible answer she could make to that statement. She just looked as Georgie chatted to Theo. Beneath her peculiar outfit, she really was very pretty. Even with the little red plastic heart stuck under her left eye she looked good. It suited her outfit.

Theo stood up like a gentleman and offered Georgie a seat. "Corrie and I were out to dinner and decided to drop in," he said. "We were with Corrie's parents, which is why we're dressed up." Corrie analyzed this new lie. It could have been worse. At least he hadn't let on they were with the mayor of New York. "So, when do you leave for the big city?" Theo asked.

"Tomorrow."

"That's nice. Where are you staying?"

"In an apartment on the East Side."

"Maybe I'll give you a call when I'm in town."

"I'll give you my number," Georgie said with a smile. "I hope you'll give me a call when you're in New York as well, Corrie," she added with equal friendliness.

Theo glowed with pleasure. He refused to see that Georgie was just a warmhearted girl, friendly with everyone.

Corrie smiled vaguely. The music started up again, and she said, "Why don't you two dance? I'm still tired from the last one."

Georgie looked at Theo's flushed face and perspiring brow. She put her hand on his wrist and said, "I'll ask them to play a slow number for you, Theo."

"Groovy," Theo smiled. He didn't catch that subtle "you," not "us."

Nothing was so pathetic as adults trying to keep up with teenage fashions and slang. Why was he doing this to himself? Love sure was blind. It made Theo mistake Georgie's thoughtfulness for love. A slow ballad began, and Georgie led Theo off to a darker corner of the room to dance. Corrie was sure she just didn't want him to be battered by the others, but he probably took it for a romantic move.

Wrapped up in the mystery of Theo's behavior, Corrie failed to see Bryan standing at the door, watching her. That dress, he thought, should be labeled "dangerous." She wasn't aware of him until he was standing beside her.

"Hi," he said.

How a man could pack so much meaning into a single syllable was really amazing. That "Hi" would take minutes to analyze. It said "Alone at last," "I'm glad you're here," "You look terrific," and a lot of other things. It was the glinting green eyes that said "I want to make love to you." Corrie felt herself blush at the message in those eyes.

"Care for something to drink?" he asked.

"Thanks. Whatever you're serving."

"Why don't you come to the bar with me and you can make your choice?"

"All right."

Bryan took her hand to help her up and held it as they left. They walked along a corridor toward a lighted room. To ease the tension, Corrie said, "This is a lovely house."

"It was my parents' home. When Dad died, we thought of selling, but I didn't think Georgie needed any more upheaval at the time. People say you shouldn't make any big decisions right after the death of a loved one. I guess they're right. I'm glad I kept the house."

They went into the lighted room, which turned out to be a den, or study. It was oak-lined, with a desk and some bookcases, as well as a sofa and TV. There was a bar along one wall.

"How long ago did your father die?" Corrie asked.

"A year ago."

"I'm sorry."

"Heart attack," he said briefly. The little tugging at the corner of his lips told her it still hurt to talk about it. "From overwork, of course. I don't plan to let it happen to me." He turned to the bar and said, "What's your poison?"

"A glass of that Chablis will do fine."

He poured two, handed her one and led her to the sofa. "Cheers," he said, and touched her glass.

A year ago was when Theo had mentioned first going out with Georgie. She frowned and said, "Isn't that—"

He nodded. "Yeah. That's when Georgie decided to make Theo her surrogate father. She'd been doing some modeling work locally. She got an interview with a bigger agency in New York, and they said she was great, but they wanted her teeth straightened. One incisor protruded a little. I thought it was kind of cute," he said with a nostalgic smile.

"And Theo did the work?"

"He did a great job on her teeth. Then they started to date a little. It's really my fault. I was so busy at work, having to take over the reins from Dad. I should have saved more time for Georgie. She was very close to Father. I knew she'd been out with her orthodontist a couple of times. She said he was a very sweet man. 'A big cuddly teddy bear' she called him. Is he?" he asked, quirking an eyebrow at her.

"It's not the way I see him."

"Well, Georgia did. The next thing I knew, she came to me and announced she was engaged—to a guy she'd been out with about five times. It was just loneliness looking for somebody to attach herself to."

Corrie listened avidly. Why was he telling her this? Bryan didn't seem the kind of man to reveal his secrets to just anyone. "What did you do? Forbid it?" she asked.

Bryan shook his head. "Oh, no. You don't 'forbid' Georgia. That would have sent her crawling out a ladder to elope with him. We're a little stubborn, we Holmes children, when it comes to getting what we want," he said. A gleam of green fire sparked from his eyes, and his lips opened in a smile that made Corrie's blood race. *And I want you*, that look said.

It was unsettling, but she enjoyed the intimacy of having Bryan to herself for a few minutes, discovering new facets to his personality. She was happy to see he could be kind and considerate when he cared deeply for someone.

"Georgie doesn't strike me as a rebellious sort. She seems very sweet."

"It was what people call 'a phase she was going through.' She's happy now, so she's sweet and demure. I confess I dread the day she comes home and introduces her next fiancé."

"You're lucky she did introduce him and not just slip off. She was probably just making a bid for attention."

"She sure as hell got it. I talked to Theo," he continued. "I tried to make him see she was reacting to her father's death. He agreed to wait a few months, and I started spending more time with her. It wasn't too hard to wean her away from him, but Theo..." Bryan shook his head in frustration.

"Maybe he really does love her," Corrie suggested reluctantly.

"He thinks so, at any rate. She hadn't seen him for months until last week at the school reunion."

"He's convinced himself she just went there to see him."

"She went to be seen—in that black dress."

"Do you think this is a good time for her to move out on her own? If she's in New York, and he calls on her—"

"She won't be on her own," he said firmly. "She's staying with her Aunt Madge, a widow who won't put up with any nonsense. I may have been derelict about Georgie before. This time I'm not taking any chances. Besides, she's all gung ho on her career now. She doesn't talk about marriage."

Corrie mulled the situation over, wondering what was the right thing to do.

"What does Dear Corrie suggest?" Bryan asked. A flickering smile touched his eyes. "Do you approve of my getting her out of town? She wants to go."

Corrie decided that Bryan was right in trying to keep Theo and Georgie apart. Georgie wasn't in love, and even if Theo rushed her into a marriage, it wouldn't last. She was too young and unsettled.

"Dear Corrie isn't an advice-to-the-lovelorn column," she pointed out. "It's my general-letter-answering column."

"Do I have to write you a letter? You're involved in this too, Corrie."

"Only peripherally. You've already told me your opinion of my advice."

His eyes studied her intently. "That was when I thought you were a girl. I can see by your dress you're all grown up, and very nicely, too."

Corrie gave him a cool look to hide the heat his words caused. "Maybe I should warn you, she's giving him her number in New York. He even mentioned moving his own practice there. The man is serious," she said.

He frowned. Why was she telling him this? Was she afraid Georgie was going to steal Theo from her? Surely a woman like Corrie didn't love Theo. She was too old to need a surrogate father, and for a lover she could do better. "I thought he was serious about *you*. The trip to Mexico, and Canada."

If this situation was ever going to be straightened out, now was the time for it. And since it was a serious matter, Corrie decided she should come clean.

She opened her mouth to confess the whole thing and closed it again. It was impossible to admit to

Bryan Holmes that she'd met Theo at a dating service. It sounded so desperate, and after all the other lies she'd been involved in he'd never believe it had anything to do with her work. But she had to tell him some part of the truth.

Then she read the sharp interest on Bryan's face. Such a mobile face, and intelligent. She wouldn't get away with half the truth. "Actually, I didn't—"

"There they are!" Georgie's high-pitched voice came to them from the doorway. Behind her stood Theo, glaring at Bryan. He let Georgie drag him forward.

"Corrie, congratulations!" Georgie said.

Corrie looked a mute and worried question at Theo. Now what had he said?

"They're getting married," Georgie announced to Bryan. "That should ease your mind, brother!"

"Married!" Bryan exclaimed. The look he turned on Corrie was not only disbelieving. It was furious.

"Theo!" Corrie exclaimed, outraged.

"We won't tell a soul," Georgie promised. "Theo told me it's a big secret. Because of Corrie's ex-fiancé," she continued, talking to her brother. "Isn't it intense, Bryan? Just like a soap opera. They don't want to embarrass the senator. Corrie just gave him back his ring last week."

Corrie could take no more. She jumped to her feet. "Theo, how dare you!"

"They won't tell," he said, giving her a look that begged for mercy.

"There's nothing to tell! It isn't true."

Theo jumped in hastily. "Actually the senator hadn't given her a ring. Corrie was going to move in with him, but they planned to get married soon. As soon as the senator could get his divorce," he added wildly.

"I was not going to move in with any senator!"

"We won't tell a soul," Georgie assured them.

"I'm sorry, darling," Theo said placatingly to Corrie. "It just slipped out, but no one will tell." He looked at Bryan and added, "She's worried what her boss will think."

Bryan bit back a sardonic laugh. "Well she might be! Helmer won't care for any scandal. He's a little old-fashioned in his morals."

"Then he'll be glad we're getting married," Theo said.

Georgie considered all this, then said, "Can I come to the wedding?"

"There isn't going to be any wedding," Corrie announced. With a hard glare at Theo she added, "A murder, possibly."

Georgie gave a gasp of horrified pleasure. "Whose?" she asked.

"Come and see for yourself," Corrie suggested. "You're all invited. We're going home, Theo. Thank you for the lovely party, Georgie. I hope you like New York. Good night, folks."

Then she strode out of the room, barely able to hold in the tears of anger and shame. She pulled the front door open for herself and walked outside. Theo came out behind her. "You forgot your coat," he said. The wind pulled at her thin dress, making her shiver.

"Never mind that. I'm not going back in there." She ran toward the car and let herself in. She was so hot with shame she didn't need her coat. Not satisfied with telling them that they toured the world together, Theo had told them she'd been on the point of shacking up with some senator. It was a wonder he hadn't used an actual name and gotten her charged with slander. How *could* he?

Theo looked like a whipped dog when he got in the car. "Corrie, I can explain everything," he said humbly.

"It better be damned good, or you're going to have some massive repair work to do on your own teeth."

Theo put his hands on the wheel and laid his head down on top of them. "Oh Corrie, I've been such a fool," he moaned. "Georgie doesn't love me at all. She never did. She was just being friendly, making a fuss over me at the reunion and dancing with me tonight. She wasn't jealous of you. She was only afraid you were using me. Bryan tried to tell me before that ꝿ she didn't love me, but I wouldn't listen. She felt sorry for me tonight. She told me I could call on her in New York, but it could only be as a friend. It was all over between us. She was at loose ends when her father died, and—I don't know. She thought of me as a safe port or something. Just someone to look after her."

Theo lifted his head. His eyes were glazed with tears. "She thought she loved me when we were engaged. Oh, I loved her so much, Corrie. She was like a bright and beautiful butterfly. I never had a girlfriend before, not a real one. Never one like Georgie. Just a few women my mother wanted me to go out with. I was never one of the popular ones at college," he admitted. "At high school they used to call me Fatty. I lost thirty pounds after I graduated," he added.

Corrie felt her anger softening to pity. How could she go on being mad at this poor soul whose heart was breaking? She could almost understand how the whole mess happened. How Georgie, young and lonesome and upset at her father's death, could imagine she loved Theo. How an unpopular man could fall in love with a beautiful woman even if she was too young for him.

She patted his arm. "It's all right, Theo. I understand. There will be another woman along. Georgie wasn't right for you."

He grabbed her hand. "I'm so ashamed of myself. And in front of you, Corrie. You're so pretty and intelligent and kind." He took her hand and held it. "It's lonesome being a bachelor at my age. I don't go out much. I tried a squash club, but I got a hernia. I went to a singles bar a couple of times. I met a woman. She had two kids with crooked teeth," he said. "She was only using me. They needed braces. That's the way the world is."

"No, it isn't like that—not all of it, Theo. You've just had bad luck. There are lots of nice women that would love to date you."

He gave her a hopeful look. His hands moved up her arms as he leaned toward her. "Do you really think so?"

"I know there are. Bette, my neighbor whom you met tonight, thought you were charming," Corrie said.

"Bette? Oh, the artist. I was sort of hoping you and I . . ."

His hands rose to her shoulders. His pale face came closer. Good Lord, he was going to kiss her. "No, no, Theo!"

In the darkness, she saw the sad look of resignation in his eyes. In a sudden spurt of pity, she placed a light peck on his cheek. "Bette is really very—"

There was a tap at the window. Looking up, she saw Bryan was standing with her coat. She opened the door and took it.

"Thanks, Bryan," she said.

Bryan's voice was cool, and the expression on his face was about as friendly as a piranha's. "I was afraid you might catch cold, but I see Theo's keeping you warm," he said.

Theo's arm had found its way to her shoulder where it rested possessively. Bryan didn't leave any time for explanations. He was already striding angrily back to his house. Well, that was the end of that. Over before it started.

Corrie drew a long sigh and said, "Let's go."

Theo started the car and drove her home.

Chapter Four

Theo was abject. He offered to call Georgie and tell her he had lied about the senator. "She already knows I'm a fool. What difference does it make if she learns I'm a liar as well?" he asked disconsolately.

Corrie only wanted to forget the whole fiasco. She wouldn't be seeing Bryan Holmes again, and that was just as well. He thought she was a phony, and she knew he was a womanizer, so what was the point? Just get on with her work and maybe just forget the escort for the office party. Her desire to take revenge on Harry Danton was beginning to seem as childish as Theo's stunts. She'd go alone, or with one of the men she was friendly with. She didn't have to impress anybody.

There were three dating services in Barton Falls. Corrie had tried two of them for the column she was writing. One more to go. If she hadn't already made a date from that service, she wouldn't have bothered to go out that Friday night. True, the new man sounded interesting. According to his file, he was an avionics engineer, never married, twenty-nine, six feet one inch tall, brown hair, liked flying, reading and jogging. And with this one last date, she'd be through with re-searching computer dating.

Bruce looked promising when she met him at the Club Tampico. The Tampico was a popular bar with a small dance floor. A good place to get acquainted, and right downtown, so catching a cab home was handy if Bruce turned out to be a dud. She always met the agency dates away from her house the first time, in case she didn't want to see them again. In Theo's case, he had seemed harmless enough and she'd let him drive her home.

Bruce was waiting for her at a table near the door. She had told him she'd wear a red jacket and dotted scarf. "Corrie James?" he asked, standing up as she went toward him.

She took in the overall impression first. The man had definite possibilities. He was handsome in the rugged, athletic style. A good physique, well-tailored sports jacket, nice brown eyes.

"I'm Bruce Longman," he said, showing her a seat. "Can I take your coat?" She shucked off her jacket, and he tossed it on the banquette. "What can I get you to drink?"

"White wine will be fine."

Before the wine even arrived, he had moved over to sit on her side of the banquette. "We don't want any-thing coming between us, right?" he asked. His eyes began examining her body in careful detail.

She moved to the farthest corner. It was a table for four, so there was plenty of room. "Your outline said you like flying, Bruce," she said matter-of-factly. "Do you have your license?"

"License? Hell, I have my own twin-engine. I'm cutting down to the Bahamas tomorrow? Care to come fly with me?"

She gave him a chilling stare. "No, thanks. I'm busy."

"Hard to get, huh?" He laughed. "I like that. I could see right off you were a bright woman."

Looking at him and realizing she'd been fooled by the first impression, Corrie doubted her own brilliance. "Sometimes I wonder," she admitted.

"Hey, it's not too late to change your mind."

"No, I'm not going to change my mind, Bruce."

"You know what you want. I like that."

The wine came. She'd drink hers up quickly and leave. "What do you read, Bruce?" she asked brightly. "Your outline mentioned reading."

"I read the comics," he said and laughed. "If you don't put something cerebral on those forms, you end up with airheads." She gave him a leery look. "But seriously, I read a lot," he added.

"I guess there are lots of comic books out there."

"How about you, Corrie?"

The best thing was to discourage him from the outset. "I read philosophy and theology."

"No kidding! Hey, I'm impressed. Do you jog?"

"No, I don't."

"Too bad. You meet a lot of nice people jogging in the park. Those short shorts and tight shirts!"

Corrie finished her wine and set her glass down. "I have to run now, Bruce. Thanks for the wine."

"Hey, we're just getting acquainted," he said and edged closer to her on the banquette. He took her hand and squeezed it.

"If you don't let go of my hand this minute, I'm going to smash that wineglass on your head," she said, smiling to conceal from the other customers that she was being hit on.

Bruce took it as a great joke. "An Irish temper! I like that!"

Was there anything this man didn't like? He sounded like a broken phonograph. "Let me out, or I'm going to scream, Bruce," she said through a clenched smile.

Something in her eyes convinced Bruce she meant it. "What did you go out with me for, if you don't like men?" he grouched and finally slid off the seat to let her out.

"I like men just fine. It's only overgrown adolescents like you I can't stand." She grabbed her coat and hurried out.

Corrie was mortified when the other customers had looked at her. One man a few seats down had even stood up, ready to help. Tonight was a definite black mark against one dating service. She'd warn her readers to check out the company before signing up. At the door she stopped to slip on her jacket. She felt someone holding it behind her and turned around to thank the waiter.

"Bryan!" she exclaimed in horror. "What are you doing here?" It was really too much! Every time she met this man she was in some dire straits. Now what would he think? That she had let a stranger try to pick her up?

"Just rescuing a damsel in distress," he answered.

Through her embarrassment Corrie noticed he was wearing a peculiar expression. There was satisfaction there in the smug set of his lips, but it was the question in his eyes that made her heart race.

"I'm fine. No trouble, but thanks," she said and turned to leave.

Bryan's hand fell on her arm and pulled her gently back. She knew her face was pink with embarrassment, but she met his steady gaze. "The night's young," he said. "Don't give up on the whole sex because one guy tried to jump you. A new acquaintance, is he?"

"You could say that."

"It might be wiser if you limit your dates to men you know a little," he suggested.

"Thanks for the advice."

"Any time, Dear Corrie."

It was all there in the ironic way he said it. A dig that a person writing on life-styles couldn't even handle her own life. There was a reminder, too, of Theo and his lies about her totally fictitious fame.

"Where's the ball and chain tonight?" he asked.

It took her a minute to figure it out. "You mean Theo?"

"Isn't he the current fiancé, or whatever you call them?"

That was a crack about the senator. How insulting he made it sound. She had had enough of men like Bruce and Theo. Enough of a playboy like Bryan Holmes intimating she was loose. Enough of the noncommittal Harry Danton types. Enough of men, period.

Fire leapt from her eyes, but her voice was like cold steel. "Trouble, I call them. And not worth it. Good night, Mr. Holmes. Don't let me keep you from your date."

She turned on her heel and marched out into the street. Bryan, wearing a grin from ear to ear, marched at her heels. "I don't have a date," he said. "This package of trouble is entirely at your disposal, Dear Corrie."

She walked faster. Bryan's long legs kept pace, without even hurrying. "Fine. Maybe you'll help me hail a cab," she said.

"I'll do better. I'll drive you home."

"I'd rather walk, through fire and noxious fumes, if necessary."

"In that case, you definitely need an escort. I seem to remember reading in the *Herald*—Dear Corrie's column, I think it was—that women shouldn't be out alone on the streets after dark."

She turned a fulminating eye on him. "You didn't read anything of the sort! The solution to muggers isn't to keep people off the streets. It's to lock up the muggers. And the same applies to women being harassed. The innocent victims aren't the ones who should be punished."

He gave her a doubtful look. "There's innocent and then there's innocent. You *did* accept a stranger's offer of a seat and a drink. What did you think he had in mind? A game of tiddledywinks?"

"He wasn't a total stranger—a pickup, if that's what you're implying. I had a date to meet him there. I just didn't know what he was like."

"We're back to square one. You shouldn't be going out with strangers."

"Don't worry. I've learned my lesson."

She saw a cab driving toward them and moved to the curb to hail it. Bryan pulled her arm down. "Do you know that cabdriver?" he asked. A grin pulled his lips back. "Getting into a car with a strange man, you never learn."

The car shot past and she scowled at Bryan. He had turned into a boy again, laughing and looking harmless. But he was obviously no kid. That cashmere jacket covered a fully mature set of shoulders. The sports shirt was open at the neck to reveal a glimpse of bronzed chest.

"What did you do that for?" she demanded.

Bryan cocked his head to one side and examined her. "You owe me an explanation. I've being going crazy trying to figure you out."

He sounded genuinely perplexed, and genuinely interested. "My car's over there," he said, pointing across the street to a little white sports car. "Don't worry," he said, when she gave him a wary look. "I'm not going to molest Fred Helmer's best-known journalist. I don't want to read about myself in the newspapers."

She gave him a steely look. Elevating her to the "best-known journalist" wasn't going to help him. "That's exactly what you'll do if you try anything."

"You think you're that irresistible, Corrie? Or do you just think I make a pass at any thing wearing a skirt? That's not very flattering to me."

He took her arm and piloted her across the street and into the car. After he had pulled smoothly into the line of traffic, he turned to her. "Your place or mine?"

The insolent question made her blood boil. "When I accept a drive home, I usually mean my home."

"Is tonight one of your exceptions? You did say usually."

"The only exception about tonight is that I wish I'd taken that cab."

He nodded. "Your place it is. The reason I gave you a choice is that we'd be chaperoned at my place. I have a housekeeper. I thought maybe a lady who had just had to fight for her virtue would prefer that."

Corrie gave him an ironic look. "Thoughtful of you."

Bryan pretended to misunderstand her tone. "It comes from having a kid sister. A brother thinks of those things."

"How is Georgie?" she asked. As soon as the question was out, she realized his trick. By bringing up Georgie, he was trying to establish that he was more than a stranger. That they had at least a few mutual friends and/or acquaintances. Talking about a man's sister seemed so normal it diluted the strained feeling of their meeting.

"She called this afternoon to say she wouldn't be home until later. It's a funny thing. Georgie's been driving me bonkers for the last couple of years, but now that she's gone the house seems empty," he replied. "I couldn't stand the silence and decided to go out for a drink."

Corrie took a quick peek at his profile and noticed his lips were set in a grim line. He actually looked lonesome. But if this was a bid for sympathy, it wasn't going to work.

"You must know half the people in Barton Falls. There's no reason for you to be by yourself. Why don't you give someone a call?"

Bryan turned his head toward her and gave an impish smile. "I did call someone," he said, "but there was no answer. You'd think a journalist would have an answering service."

"You called me?" In spite of herself she was flattered.

He hunched his shoulders. "I figured it was worth a shot. And if you were really serious about Theo, all you had to do was say no. Can I assume that it's over between you two, or do you have that anomaly, an open relationship, with him?"

The car was heading west. It passed Mountainview Road, where it should have turned north to reach Corrie's apartment. "Hey, where are you going?" she demanded.

"You didn't tell me where you live. You weren't interested in going to my place, so I thought we'd settle for neutral territory. That's what the diplomats do when they're trying to establish a truce. What do you say we go to the Old Mill? They have a good selection of wine. A nice chilled Chablis," he tempted.

Corrie felt a little thrill of triumph that he remembered what she'd been drinking. She was all dressed up for a date. It was Friday night, and the alternative was to go home. But she knew herself well enough to know that all of the above were just rationales. Every atom of her body wanted to be with him. She enjoyed the challenge, the excitement of crossing swords with this man.

"All right. One drink," she said primly. When she glanced at him, she saw the quick smile that flickered across his face.

"You didn't answer my question about Theo," he reminded her. "Is it all over between you two?"

"Yes," seemed the easiest answer. Why go into all the bizarre details of that business? "It's all over."

"Good." The smile was back. This time it was more than a passing flicker.

Bryan changed the subject immediately. As they drove north beyond the city limits, he talked about the new factories that had been built there. It passed the time until they reached the Old Mill. The restaurant and tavern had been converted from a derelict lumber mill. The sprawling old stone building that rose from the banks of the Barton River wasn't exactly beautiful, but it had a certain austere distinction and the charm of yesterday.

The decor was what Bette would call "early nostalgia." The chintz curtains and hooked rugs in the lobby suggested colonial days. In the main room, bits of Americana decorated the walls, and at the end of the room a huge fireplace cast a golden glow on the furnishings. Corrie found it impossible not to feel friendlier toward mankind in this cosy spot. Bryan had probably chosen it for that very reason, she reminded herself.

"Do you want to sit near the fire?" he asked.

"I'd love to."

He spoke to the maître d' by name. Although the fireplace seats were taken, the owner of Holmes Chemical Plant had no trouble. Two chairs and a low table were squeezed in. Bryan ordered the Chablis. When it arrived, Corrie saw he had ordered a whole bottle. She didn't say anything, but her expression reminded him she had specified one drink.

The waiter poured a little into Bryan's glass. He tasted it and nodded, then the waiter filled both glasses and left.

Bryan lifted his glass in salute. "A toast?" he suggested. "To peace in the war between the sexes."

The flickering flames played over his golden hair and bronzed face. In this dim light, his eyes looked like emeralds, and there was laughter lurking at the corners of his lips. Bryan Holmes could be almost irresistible when he wanted to, and now he was going to start trying to charm her. Alarm bells went off in Corrie's head.

"Let's make that a truce," she parried.

"Spoken like a true diplomat," he said, and drank.

They settled in, looking around at the place and the customers. "I used to bring Georgie here," Bryan said. "When she first wanted to start acting grown-up, you know."

"You seem to be very close to your sister."

"It's my guilty conscience. I didn't realize how lonesome she was until the Theo affair."

"Didn't she have any friends?"

"Lots of them, but what she needed was parents. Mom died when Georgie was thirteen, just at the age when a girl needs her mother most. Aunt Madge wanted to take her, but Dad and I, in our wisdom, thought it was better for her to be at home.''

"You needed someone, too,'' Corrie pointed out.

He nodded pensively. "Yes, I think that was why we did it—selfishness.''

Corrie felt a troublesome urge to defend him. "It's only natural. Besides, she didn't come to any real harm.''

"It was close, though. Theo Manville, Lord, I don't know what she saw in—'' He came to an abrupt, conscious stop. "Sorry, I'm talking to the wrong lady on that subject.''

The wine and firelight and this more vulnerable side of Bryan's personality conspired to soften Corrie. She actually found herself feeling sorry for him. "I was never engaged to Theo,'' she said.

Bryan's eyebrows quirked up and he looked at her in disbelief. "I see. I did wonder when I saw you come into the Tampico alone tonight.''

She knew by his expression that he was leaping wildly to all the wrong conclusions. Theo had said that she'd gone to Mexico with him and was planning to go to Canada. If Bryan thought on top of that, that she'd gone to the Tampico to get picked up... She knew that it shouldn't matter to her, but it did.

"As I said, I had arranged to meet Bruce at the club. I'm doing research for my column,'' she added quickly.

"You don't review the clubs, do you?''

"No, I wasn't doing the Tampico. It was for a column I'm doing on the dating services in town. There's a lot of interest in computer dating. Of course I've read all the research, but firsthand information is the best so I decided to try it myself. Mr. Helmer thought it was a good idea. In fact, the *Herald* footed the bill.''

Bryan frowned, not in disapproval, but in concern. Helmer should have his head examined, exposing this kid to such danger. "Bighearted of them," he said angrily. "Were your other dates as interesting as this Bruce guy?''

"They were different," she said uncertainly. "I met quite a nice man who teaches English at the high school.''

"How do they match you up?''

"That's the clue to the whole thing," she said, eager to explain. "They go by what you tell them, and if the applicant lies, well, that's where it breaks down. And people don't always tell the truth. It's kind of like our clothes, you know. We tend to dress for what we want to be, and on those applications people idealize themselves. Bruce, for instance, put down that he likes to read so he'd meet intelligent women. Why he'd want anyone with a brain is beyond me, but I think what he meant is that he wanted to look intellectual himself.''

Bryan listened, nodding. "That's a pretty sharp insight," he complimented.

"I'm acquiring the knack of mind reading. I talk things like this over with the consulting psychologist. I've just given you my interpretation.''

"I see I'll have to watch my p's and q's—to say nothing of my jackets and shirts. What do my clothes reveal?''

It gave Corrie an excuse to study him. "That tailor-made cashmere jacket suggests a few things: you like the best, you like luxury. Cashmere is so soft," she added with a sigh. "And the fact that it's not off the rack tells me you treasure your uniqueness. You want to tell the world you're you. It also says you have a fair bit of money, and very good taste in my opinion," she added, with a smile.

"But now you're saying the clothes tell you what I am, not what I want to be."

She thought for a moment. "It's mostly ambitious, aspiring people that dress for what they want to be. If you already are what you aspire to, then you just dress accordingly."

"I tremble to think what my sister's weird and wonderful wardrobe reveals. Do you think she has a secret desire to be a cartoon character?" he mused. Despite his harsh suggestion, he smiled fondly.

Bryan was still smiling when he turned his attention to Corrie's clothing. She had put her red jacket and dotted scarf on the back of her chair. Her simple navy dress looked plain without them.

A glimmer of mischief sparked in his eyes. "And you, Corrie, do you really aspire to be a nun?" he asked.

His close examination made her nervous. She fidgeted with the sleeves of her dress. "I hadn't planned to take off my jacket. Nuns don't wear bright red jackets."

"Not according to Freud," he teased. "Red is for hot-blooded, passionate women. It inspires men with all sorts of ideas."

"Maybe that's why I took it off when we came in," she joked. "I wouldn't want to give you the wrong idea about me."

"Here I thought it was just the heat from the fireplace."

There was enough heat coming from the conversation that Corrie was eager to divert it. "I usually wear suits or tailored clothes to work."

"Dress for success, huh? That shiny red dress you wore to the school reunion wasn't tailored. Red again. I think you'd better have Doc Bankes take a closer look into your psyche. It's trying to tell you something."

Corrie noticed that he even knew the name of the consulting psychologist the *Herald* used. "That particular purchase was my bankbook talking. The dress was on sale."

Bryan laughed. "Whatever else you are, you sure as hell are a woman! Georgie goes ape at the sight of a sale sign."

Corrie was surprised to find herself talking so easily to him. She'd thought the president of Holmes Chemical would be snooty. She hardly noticed when he lifted the wine bottle and filled her glass again.

"We really should eat something with this," he suggested. "I wouldn't want the wine going to your head. They have some good finger food here."

He called the waiter, and soon a plate of chicken wings and deep-fried potato skins were on the table between them. The aroma rose enticingly to her nostrils and she picked up a wing.

"Fried," she said. "It's not good for us, but it looks delicious."

"A bird in the hand should be fried. Otherwise, you use a fork. They're spicy," he warned.

They were obviously doused in Tabasco or cayenne, but they were delicious, and the wine helped cool her throat. The wine in the bottle sank lower and the full plate gradually emptied as they talked. Bryan asked her about her career plans. Corrie explained that her life-styles work was a foot in the door. She did features as well, and eventually she'd make it to the front page, if she was good enough.

Bryan told her a little about his chemical plant. He'd majored in organic chemistry at college, but now he didn't get much chance to use it. There was too much administrative work to do since his father's death. After an hour's leisurely conversation, one lone chicken wing sat on the plate.

"You have it," she said. "I won't be able to get into my clothes if I eat any more."

His eyes flickered approvingly over her dress. "There's room for one more wing," he said with a smile. "Personally I have nothing against a woman with a little meat on her bones. Georgie weighs about ten pounds, and since she got with this modeling agency, all she does is worry about gaining a gram."

Georgie again. He was certainly a concerned brother. Bryan noticed the look she gave him and laughed. "I don't really think I'm her father. I just worry about her, that's all. Now that my little sister's out in the big bad world, I'm readjusting my thinking about how men treat women."

"A playboy," Theo had called him. "A macho man." How he treated women himself was what Bryan meant, and his memories obviously worried him.

"At least Theo's intentions were honorable," he said pensively. He frowned as he studied Corrie.

She was coming to know him well enough to attempt reading his mind. Georgie hadn't run off to Mexico with him before they were married, like she was supposed to have done. She didn't want Bryan to have that opinion of her, and to correct it, she had to dispel the rumor.

"Theo's just a big kid," she said. "He only spouted all that foolishness about our having met in Mexico and my being a magazine reporter to make Georgie jealous. I only met him a few days before the school reunion. He was one of the men I met when I was researching the computer dating business."

Bryan's frown disappeared and a wicked smile replaced it. "Well, I'll be a son of a gun. I should have known it! Theo was always a dope. He used to carry a picture of a buxom blonde in a bikini in his wallet at school. He said she was his girlfriend from California, but she never appeared in person. We always suspected he'd just snapped a picture of some girl at the beach."

"That sounds like Theo," she admitted ruefully.

"So you were never his—"

"No, I wasn't," she said firmly. "I was just a phony, like the blonde in his wallet. He's finally realized your sister doesn't care about him. I don't think he'll give you any more trouble."

Bryan seemed pleased to hear it. There was a gleam of real satisfaction in his eyes. "Well, this has been quite a night," he said and thoughtlessly picked up the last chicken wing. "Sorry! I offered that to you."

"There's room in your jacket for another half an ounce," she said.

"I'll let you have the dregs of the wine." He lifted the bottle to pour the last inch.

Corrie covered her glass with her hand. "I've had my limit. We'd better be going." She glanced at her watch. "Good heavens! It's eleven o'clock! We've been here nearly two hours."

"Do you turn into a pumpkin at midnight?"

"No, into a working girl at seven-thirty tomorrow morning."

"The more I hear about your job, the more I think Helmer's exploiting you." He drank the last of the wine and helped her on with her jacket, smiling at its fire-engine color. No thoughts of scarlet women were in his mind. It was the bright, youthful sort of thing his sister liked.

Corrie would probably have a fit if he said what he was thinking. That in some peculiar way, Corrie reminded him of Sis. They were both young, with the sort of vulnerable innocence masquerading as worldliness that made him want to protect them, although that wasn't his first reaction to Corrie James. Lord, he must be getting old.

He paid the bill and they left. "Home, James? Ms. James, that is," he joked.

"Home, Holmes," she replied, and laughed. It was the wine that made her feel giddy.

Her throaty gurgle sent a thrill coursing through Bryan's blood. Control yourself, he said mentally. She's just a kid. Dropping Corrie James at her door wasn't what Bryan had intended when he picked her up, but a change had occurred while they were at the Old Mill.

It was thinking of his sister that did it, of course. It really worried him, sending her off to wicked New York. A model would meet all kinds of men. But Aunt Madge would be a good watchdog. She was strict without being tiresome.

Corrie gave him directions and the little white sports car pulled up in front of her apartment building. She still felt somewhat giddy from the wine. She assumed Bryan would try to kiss her good-night and planned to give him one kiss. In fact, she looked forward to it, but if he invited himself in, she'd say no.

One kiss in the car or outside her door would be safe enough. She peered through the shadows at his profile as he turned off the engine. He looked irresistible. The sculpture of his strong, straight nose was exciting. The harsh, masculine planes of his chin and jaw were limned in the lamplight. And his lips—they were quite full, sensual. Her own lips tingled as she thought that soon she'd feel those warm lips pressing on hers. A macho man—that's what he looked like all right. A very attractive macho man.

Her heart began speeding up as she waited for him to turn and make a move. He turned away from her, opened his door and got out to open hers. He must think she was going to ask him in. No way. She got out wordlessly. In perfect silence he accompanied her to the front door of her building.

"Got your key?" he asked.

She rifled in her purse and found it. "Right here," she said.

He took the key, opened the door and handed the key back. He'd either kiss her or try to follow her in. Maybe he meant to accompany her up in the elevator. It would be more private inside. There was no harm in letting him take her to her door. She walked in and looked over her shoulder, expecting to see him behind her. He was still at the door, holding it open.

"I had a swell time, Corrie," he said. "Thanks."

She blinked in surprise. Was this it? No kiss? Her eyes gazed into his a moment, looking an invitation. Then they lowered to study his lips.

Bryan watched her, reading her thoughts as clearly as if she'd spoken them. That look was an invitation. Her lips, pouting now, were an even stronger one. Lord, he wanted to taste them. He smiled uncertainly. "Why don't I give you a call sometime?" he said and immediately regretted it. Not her! Not this one. She was too pretty and too innocent. He'd end up doing something he shouldn't and feel guilty for months.

"When?" she asked.

There was definitely an invitation in those stormy gray eyes. He felt himself weaken. "I'm pretty busy next week."

"Oh." The invitation dwindled to a question. "When will I hear from you then?"

"I'll call you. Okay?"

The questioning look congealed to annoyance. "Sure," she said tightly. "Give me a buzz some time you have nothing better to do. Thanks for the wine, Bryan. It was fun." She marched angrily off toward the elevators.

Bryan let the door close and stood looking in through the glass at her retreating figure. She still had the cutest tush in town. He had definitely done the right thing, the gentlemanly thing, in letting her escape. So why did he feel like a very dissatisfied jerk? It was the accusation in those innocent gray eyes. Ironically, she was accusing him for not doing what he wanted very much to do—to pull her into his arms and kiss her until her toes curled.

He muttered an accomplished curse under his breath and returned to his car.

Chapter Five

It had been nearly a week since Corrie had seen Bryan. She'd spent five days waiting for the phone to ring. Surely he'd call. He said he would, and he had seemed to like her. Corrie was reluctant to leave the office in case he phoned. She didn't even like to leave her desk. She had an article ready for the proofreader but decided to wait for Joe, the office boy, to pick it up on his rounds.

She did have to leave her desk once to get information on a Miss Thorndyke from the newspaper "morgue." Corrie always disliked to enter that room where obituaries on important living people were kept up to date, to have the information assembled in case of a sudden death. Presidents and monarchs and movie stars—all their obituaries were there.

On Thursday, Mr. Helmer asked her to do a feature article on Miss Isobel Thorndyke. The woman wasn't a national celebrity, but in Barton Falls she was important enough to be included in the morgue. She'd taught public school there for forty years. Corrie took the file to her desk and read it.

It seemed a shame that a woman who had worked so long in town couldn't seem more real to her. She went to the photo files and found a picture of Miss Thorndyke. It was hard to tell what she looked like from the photographic plate. She looked severe, with her hair scooped back in a knot. Her eyes, though, looked wise and kind.

Corrie talked to some of the local people at the office. "Old Thorney dead?" they said and shook their heads. They only remembered that she'd been "kind of strict, but a good teacher." It made Corrie think of her own school days and inevitably of death.

She sat at her word processor and began to write the article. Her expression was sad, trying to breathe life into this article on a stranger. Miss Thorndyke was still single when she died at age seventy-one. What a lonesome, narrow life the woman must have led.

Corrie wasn't looking at the door when Bryan entered. He saw her from across the room and felt his pulse quicken at the sight. When he thought of Corrie, and he thought of her more than he liked, he remembered her sitting across from him at the Old Mill on Friday night. Her eyes had danced with pleasure then. What made her so sad now?

Bryan was already late for his appointment with Mr. Helmer but he stopped at her desk in passing and glanced at the screen. Corrie saw his shadow and handed him her copy without looking up. "I want a three-column header on this, Joe," she said.

"Cut to the quick!" Bryan said. "You don't even remember my name."

At the sound of his familiar voice, she gave a jump of alarm. "Bryan!" she exclaimed much too loud. A smile of delight beamed. He had come here to see her in person! "It's nice to see you again."

"You took the words right out of my mouth. I was eavesreading over your shoulder. I see you're doing a eulogy on Miss Thorndyke."

"Trying to," she said, glancing at her inauspicious beginning. "They want forty inches. I'm having trouble getting twenty."

Bryan looked surprised. "Good Lord, you can't have known her very well. No, of course you wouldn't know her at all. You didn't go to school here."

"Did you know her?" Corrie asked hopefully.

"Know her?" he asked and laughed ruefully. "I loved her. She was a great old lady, and I do mean lady."

"I wish you'd tell me something about her."

Bryan looked at his watch. "I didn't really come here to be interviewed. I'm in a bit of a rush."

"Oh!" Corrie waited, expecting he'd rush on to ask her for a date.

"What the heck, I can spare a few minutes for Old Thorney," he decided and drew up a chair. "She was my teacher when I was in grade eight. Thorney taught the four R's."

"You mean three R's."

"Four," he insisted. "Reading, 'Riting, 'Rithmetic and Righteousness. She threw in a little morality while she was at it. I guess that's what made her so special.

She really cared about us young whelps." His voice was gentle with memories.

Corrie hesitated to speak, he looked so pre-occupied. She had never seen Bryan in this mood before, so serious and so sad. "Could you give me a 'for instance'?" she asked.

He drew himself back to attention. "For instance, the time she caught me and some of my friends smoking in the school basement."

"You!" Corrie exclaimed.

Bryan tossed up his hands. "I never said I was perfect. Anyway, it was my last year of public school. Three of us were in the basement supposedly putting the sports equipment away on the very last day. I guess it took us a little longer than it should have. Thorney came slipping downstairs, quiet as a mouse. I'll never forget it. We managed to get the cigarettes hidden, but I suppose the air was blue. I felt as if one of the Apostles had caught me doing something wrong. She had that kind of moral imperative about her."

"What did she say?" Corrie demanded.

"Nothing, at first. Not a word. She just held out her hand, and I, being the ringleader, put the package of cigarettes in it."

"We'll discuss this after class is dismissed, gentlemen," she said then. "She usually called us 'boys,' but by calling us 'gentlemen,' she was letting us know we were old enough to take responsibility."

"And since it was the last day of school, it didn't leave her much time to punish you," Corrie said. "What did she do?"

"She asked us how *we* thought we should make recompense for behaving badly behind our parents' backs. You can imagine how that casual mention of 'parents' struck us dumb."

"Did she tell your parents?"

"No, she dumped the whole responsibility on us, where it belonged. But she let us know a wrong had to be paid off with a right. The three of us ended up volunteering to mow the grass at the school all summer. There was a janitor, but he had plenty else to keep him busy. She instilled a sense of responsibility and did it while still making you feel good about yourself. When she left the school, I remember we felt about ten feet tall. We were *men*, we could take our punishment. We weren't just kids any longer."

Corrie nodded thoughtfully. "She sounds like a wise lady."

"Kind too. She lived right beside the school, and she always had a bottle of soda pop for us after the lawn was mowed. That kind of caring is hard to find nowadays. Barton Falls owes a lot to Old Thorney."

"My Dad was something like that," Corrie said.

Bryan gave her a peculiar look. It was intimate, yet distant. She waited expectantly to hear what he'd say next. He still hadn't mentioned anything about a date.

So that's where Corrie got her high morals, Bryan thought. Old Thorney would have something to say if he started anything with a woman like Corrie. How could you make right a wrong of that magnitude? "I'm not surprised," he said and stood up.

"Well, it was nice chatting with you, Corrie. Actually, my visit here has to do with Miss Thorndyke. Helmer and I are starting up a subscription fund in her name. We want to endow a scholarship for a deserving student. Old Thorney would like that better than anything else."

"Oh!" The disappointed syllable was out before Corrie had time to prevent it.

Bryan looked at her and read the knowledge in her eyes, and the hurt. His departure had the speed of an escape. "I've got to dash. Helmer's waiting. Bye, Corrie."

"Goodbye, Bryan."

Corrie was stunned when he left. He hadn't come to see her at all! He was probably sorry he'd had to talk to her. Yet he could have gotten to Helmer's office without her noticing him. He'd gone out of his way to stop at her desk, but within five minutes he was embarrassingly eager to get away. The whole visit puzzled her, but some good had come of it.

When Corrie returned to her writing, she felt she knew Miss Thorndyke better. Bryan had helped her there. She even felt she knew Bryan a little better. It took a sound, thoughtful person to appreciate someone like Miss Thorndyke.

Corrie finished the article and returned the file to the morgue. When she got back to her desk, Bryan had left. She knew because Mr. Helmer came and told her to include the subscription fund in her article. "Mr. Holmes was just here," he mentioned.

After work on Thursday evening, Bette asked Corrie over for a final viewing of Kathy's Kittens before they were sent off to New York. The paintings had been examined and approved, and they were discussing Bryan. "I just don't understand," Corrie said.

"What would Doc Bankes advise a woman to do if she had this problem?" Bette asked.

"To phone him, of course," Corrie replied at once. "There's no reason why we have to sit waiting for men to ask us out nowadays."

Bette gave her a peculiar look. "So what's the problem? The man hasn't got a phone? Call him and ask him out."

"Of course he has." Corrie looked uncertainly at the phone. "No, I'll give him a free rein."

"Give a man enough rope and he'll skip," Bette warned.

"The problem is, I'm afraid he'll say no, and I'll feel like an idiot."

"Now we know how men have felt all these years, with the dubious privilege of phoning us." Bette laughed. "Speaking of men, did I tell you Theo's taking me to dinner tonight?"

"Again!"

Bette fluffed out her blond hair and smiled with satisfaction. "To be fair, I took him out the last time, to the art exhibition at the Montrose Gallery. He has good taste in art."

"Of course he has. He bought one of yours, or are you exchanging it for the retainer?"

"I took cash. I figure if something comes along to interrupt our romance, I can always use the retainer as an excuse to go and see him professionally."

"You're a schemer, Bette Sanderson."

"I should hope so. I'm not a daughter of Eve for nothing." Bette gave her friend a knowing look. "I like Theo a lot. Inside that childish exterior, there's a nice man trying to get out. When he makes it, I plan to be there to grab him. You have to work on these things. Dr. Bankes might recommend that a forgotten woman just pick up the phone and call the forgetter, but I notice you're too bright to take the advice."

"I'm a dyed-in-the-wool emotional coward."

"If you want my advice," Bette suggested, "forget phoning him. That's too obvious for us proud ladies. Arrange an accidental meeting."

"I don't want to go to the Tampico alone again," Corrie said, frowning.

"I didn't mean the Tampico. You want something more subtle than that. Where else does he go in the evening?"

"I don't know," Corrie admitted.

"There must be some place he'd be that you could go and meet him, accidentally on purpose."

"The only place I know for sure he goes to is work, and I can hardly turn up there accidentally."

"Why not?" Bette asked and laughed. "Faint heart never won fair hunk."

Corrie gave her a derisive look. "Be reasonable."

"Why settle for just reasonable? Be creative. Ask your boss to let you do a story on Holmes Chemical. You've been with the paper a couple of years now. It's time you hit up Helmer for a special."

"I don't know anything about chemicals."

"A good point," Bette admitted but she soon bounced back with another idea. "Holmes employ women, don't they?"

"I imagine so."

"And you're working up a series of columns on interesting women doing interesting work in Barton Falls. Ravishingly intriguing ladies like artists," she added with a blatant hint.

"I was going to do you this week," Corrie said.

"Make it next week. Do I have to draw you a picture?" Bette challenged.

"Hmm." Corrie rubbed her chin and considered this suggestion. "You mean do someone from Holmes Chemical. Not a bad idea."

"It's a great idea, and for heaven's sake get busy on it soon. The office party's in two weeks."

The office party. Corrie had practically forgotten it. Showing Harry and her workmates that she had a better man than the one she'd lost didn't seem that important anymore. She just wanted to see Bryan again.

Corrie left to let Bette get ready for her date and went back to her own apartment. Tomorrow she'd call the personnel department at Holmes Chemical and find out what women there were doing interesting jobs. If there was a chemist or chemical technologist or something, she'd go to the plant and interview her. Maybe, just maybe, Bryan would chance by.

And what if he didn't? She'd have the interview, which she did want, but she wanted more to see Bryan again. She could suggest that the interviewee ask for her boss's permission before meeting her. Then at least Bryan would know she was coming.

Corrie's spirits sank to hear that the only female chemist at Holmes Chemical was away on her annual vacation for two weeks. Is fate trying to tell me something, she wondered. She was just about to thank the personnel manager and hang up when it occurred to her that the woman talking to her had an interesting job. She hadn't done a column on a personnel manager before.

"Would you be interested in giving me an interview, Ms. Walker?" Corrie asked.

"I'd be delighted," Ms. Walker replied.

"You'll get Mr. Holmes's permission first, I assume? I wouldn't want to do it without his knowledge."

"I'll certainly tell him, but that won't be any problem. Mr. Holmes is always happy to get favorable publicity. He runs a good company here."

"That's wonderful. You'll let him know I'm coming then."

"I'll tell him. When will you be here, Ms. James?"

"The sooner the better. How about tomorrow morning around ten?"

"Can you make it ten-thirty? I have a short meeting with the department heads at ten."

"I'll be there."

Corrie assumed the meeting must have been very short. She arrived a few minutes early, and Ms. Walker was waiting for her. The personnel manager had the sleek look of a professional businesswoman. Her dark hair was short and neat. She wore a quietly elegant suit, and the dark-rimmed glasses added a touch of authority. Corrie had her camera and took a few shots before starting the interview.

Ms. Walker had an interesting job and explained her duties in some detail. She managed to work in a few plugs for the company along the way.

Corrie kept glancing to Ms. Walker's door from time to time, hoping to see Bryan. Eventually it was noon, the interview was over and he still hadn't showed up.

"Well, if that's all, Ms. James, you must excuse me now," Ms. Walker said. "I'm having a business lunch with Bryan—that's Mr. Holmes. I have to meet him at his office at noon. Can't keep the boss waiting."

She rose and shook Corrie's hand. Corrie swallowed her disappointment and left the office. So that was that. Bryan knew she was there and hadn't bothered walking a few yards down the hall to see her.

The halls were busy with people rushing from their offices to the cafeteria or home for lunch. Corrie, lugging her purse and camera, was fully occupied avoiding the traffic. This time she did see Bryan coming, spotting him just entering the front door, before he saw her. His head was down, and he was scowling. She was relieved to know he'd been out. Perhaps if he'd been in his office, he'd have dropped in to see her.

Just as they drew near, Bryan lifted his head and saw her. His scowl changed to a quick flash of surprise, then a wide smile of welcome broke. "You're still here!" he said. "I thought you'd have left by now."

Corrie glowed at his joyful welcome. She saw the pleasure shining in his eyes and the very real, warm smile. "As you can see, I'm trying to get out," she replied.

"Jan should have told you not to try to leave at noon."

Bryan put his hand on her elbow and drew her aside to an open doorway, out of the traffic. They didn't enter the room but just stepped in to avoid being trampled. The sudden sense of intimacy in the midst of so many people was peculiar. Just inches beyond there was a steady stream of bodies, but Corrie felt as if she and Bryan were alone on a desert island.

His hand was still unnecessarily resting on her elbow, but he didn't remove it. His gaze never left her face. It moved slowly from her eyes to her lips, wandered to her hair for a moment, then back to her eyes. He glanced at the open door. Was he going to close it? Corrie felt her blood quicken.

"Jan Walker told me you were coming," he said, but the words hardly mattered. They were only a vehicle for the warmth of his voice.

Was that why he had been rushing back, afraid he'd missed her? "I thought I should have your approval."

"You have!" The quick exclamation hung heavy on the air, full of suggestion. "For the interview, I mean," he added, then frowned. "Not that I mean to imply..." Bryan cleared his throat rather nervously.

Bryan Holmes nervous? "You have my approval, too," she said with a teasing smile. "For the way you treat your female employees, I mean."

Their eyes met for one intense instant of mutual recognition. I'm going to kiss her, Bryan thought. He felt an overwhelming urge to pull her into his arms, and she knew it. Her full lips were parted in anticipation.

"How did the article on Miss Thorndyke go?" His voice was less tender now. It was uncertain, hovering between intimacy and business.

When Corrie answered, she purposely used an inviting tone. "Fine. I used your line about the four R's. I hope you don't mind."

She felt his fingers tighten on her arm. "Feel free."

Now was the moment he should make his move. Why didn't he? Corrie's tone was less inviting than before. "I mentioned the subscription fund. They're taking donations at the *Herald*."

"We're taking donations here, too. A lot of employees had Miss Thorndyke for a teacher."

Why are we talking about Miss Thorndyke? This time it was Corrie who glanced at the door. Already the crowd was thinning to a trickle.

Bryan's hand fell from her elbow, and the smile in his eyes faded to impatience. "It looks as if you might make it to your car without being stampeded now."

The roller coaster of emotion left Corrie angry. "I'll risk it," she snipped and turned sharply away from Bryan, still half expecting he'd stop her.

"I'm late for a luncheon appointment. Nice bumping into you, Corrie."

She left without saying goodbye. Bryan watched grimly as she hurried toward the door. Why couldn't he have come five minutes later? Why did he have to meet her again? Corrie James was beginning to get under his skin in a way no woman had done before. He shook his head and went toward his office.

Corrie threw her camera on the car seat and violently rammed the key into the ignition. She'd had enough of Bryan Holmes ying-yanging her around. She was the one who was supposed to be playing hard to get! How dare he look at her as though he could hardly keep his hands off her, then talk about Miss Thorndyke?

She'd just forget him. He was too complicated to bother with.

Chapter Six

Corrie spent Friday afternoon composing the article on Jan Walker for Saturday's edition. It would run on the women's page with a photograph. The next day was Corrie's Saturday off. She slept in, and when the paper arrived she took it to the table to read while she had coffee. She opened it to the women's page first. Her columns never seemed quite real to her until she saw them set in print.

It was a good article, she thought. When the phone rang, Corrie jumped a foot. Bryan! was the first thing that entered her head. He was phoning to thank her for the column...and maybe to ask her out? Stop being such a fool, she chided herself.

But her voice was a little breathless when she lifted the receiver. "Hello."

"Good morning, Ms. James. It's Jan Walker. I've

just been reading your column. I think you did a lovely job and called to thank you."

Corrie's heart settled down to normal. "Thank you, Ms. Walker."

"Please call me Jan."

"I'm glad you liked it, Jan. I couldn't have done a good job without your help. You practically wrote it for me. You may have noticed how many of your quotes I used."

"And got them all right! That's unusual. I'm having a little party tonight at my place—just an informal get-together. I was wondering if you'd like to drop in."

Corrie hesitated a moment. "Let me check my calendar," she said. But it was her heart she checked. Maybe Bryan would be there. If he wasn't, an informal party with a bunch of people she didn't know wasn't Corrie's favorite way of spending an evening.

Corrie wavered, then did glance at her calendar and saw the name Jeff scrawled across Saturday. Of course, she was going to a movie with Jeff Williams. That settled it.

"Sorry, Jan. I'm busy. I have a date tonight."

"Oh, that's all right. I just thought I'd ask since we were talking. We'll do lunch some day."

"That will be fine. Thanks for calling."

"I'll be in touch next week."

Corrie hung up the phone and tried to forget the call. It proved impossible. Maybe she should have gone to Jan's party. She could have taken Jeff and let Bryan see there were other men in her life. She reached for the phone, then pushed it farther away. No, she'd done her part in chasing him. He hadn't called, so obviously he didn't want to see her. She wouldn't throw herself at him anymore. With a vague memory of Theo, she knew how unwelcome a persistent pursuer could be and how pitiable they looked.

Saturday passed quickly with all her housekeeping and shopping chores. Jeff Williams was a nice, uncomplicated date, and the movie was an amusing crime caper. It was on the tip of Corrie's tongue to ask Jeff to the office party—just two weeks away now but something held her back.

On Sunday morning, Bette dropped in for coffee.

"Where did you and Theo go last night?" Corrie asked.

"Dinner at the Estaminet and to the Old Mill after for a drink."

"The Estaminet! Fancy!"

"Theo had never been there. Neither had I actually." Bette laughed. "It costs a fortune. But why hadn't Theo ever gone before? He's just like a kid," Bette smiled fondly. "I think he's falling in love with me."

Studying her friend's glowing eyes, Corrie said, "I think maybe the feeling is mutual."

"You're right. He's such a sweet guy, Corrie. He thinks I'm doing him a big favor by going out with him. Oh, he's kind of stuffy looking, but he wants to be with it."

"I remember him trying to dance with Georgie."

Bette picked up her cup nonchalantly and said, "Did I mention Georgie was at the Old Mill last night?"

"Really! How did Theo act?"

"As if he hardly remembered her at first. But she came over and chatted, and he behaved very well. He was cool for a while but he soon broke down and was friendly. He didn't claim I was Picasso's long-lost daughter or anything like that, so I guess he's over trying to impress Georgie. She was with her brother. That Bryan's something, isn't he?"

Corrie choked on her coffee. "Bryan was there last night!"

"Yes, they'd been to a movie and drove out for a drink after."

"I thought he'd be at the party with Jan Walker."

"The lady you did the column on. No, he didn't mention her at all."

Corrie furrowed her brow in thought. If Bryan was free on a Saturday night to take his kid sister out, it looked as though he wasn't involved with anyone. But he still wasn't interested in her, either.

"I take it nothing came of your trip to Holmes Chemical?" Bette asked.

"Zip. I bumped into Bryan just as I was leaving. He had to dash off to lunch."

"He was probably busy."

"He wasn't busy last night."

"What's your next move?"

"No more moves. I wouldn't want to give him the idea I'm desperate."

"Theo and I are driving up to Vermont today to see the leaves," Bette said. "They're so beautiful this time of year. I've always felt the urge to paint them—an interpretation I mean—but they look too unreal, whole forests of red and orange and yellow."

"Theo again! This is starting to look serious."

Bette crossed her fingers and smiled. "Wish me luck, Corrie. I'm bringing him home for dinner at my place afterward. I've baked an apple pie. Can you believe it?"

"Poor Theo." Corrie laughed. "He's the one I should wish luck if he has to eat one of your leather crusts."

"I bought the crust frozen. I'm not a complete sadist. See you tomorrow."

"We'll do your interview for the column."

"Right. Bye." Bette was just leaving when the phone rang.

"Corrie?"

She recognized Bryan's voice immediately and her fingers tensed on the phone. "Yes, this is Corrie."

"Bryan Holmes here."

Corrie's heart went into palpitations. "Bryan!" she exclaimed in a fair imitation of mild interest. "How are you?"

"Just fine, thanks. I called to thank you for the complimentary article in yesterday's paper."

"You don't have to thank me. It was really a column about professional women in the community. Jan Walker's already called."

He laughed lightly. "All right, so it was an excuse."

"Why did you think you needed an excuse?"

There was a short pause, and when Bryan spoke he ignored the question. "I was hoping we could get together. Are you busy this afternoon?"

A little curl of excitement tightened in her chest. She had said she wouldn't chase him. That didn't mean she had to say no if he was doing the chasing. "I have nothing urgent planned," she said. "What did you have in mind?"

"It's such a lovely day, I thought we might just drive out in the country and admire the fall leaves. Maybe have dinner somewhere."

"That sounds fine."

"I'll pick you up about one, if that's okay."

"Great. I'll be ready."

Corrie hung up the phone and a broad smile broke. She suppressed the urge to jump up and down and shout for joy. It worked after all. The interview had brought a call, even if it took longer than she hoped. Whatever had caused Bryan's reserve earlier, he wanted to see her now.

It was Theo who had misled her. He gave her the idea Bryan was a playboy, when he was really rather shy. An excuse to call, he'd said.

A peaceful afternoon's drive through the countryside admiring the flamboyant colors of autumn was a good chance to become better acquainted. Maybe they'd get out and walk through a forest, hand in hand. Dinner after at some romantic spot by candlelight....

Now what should she wear? There was a nip in the air. She'd wear slacks and boots and a warm sweater, but that didn't mean she had to look grungy. Corrie chose her navy plaid slacks and a navy sweater. A big red wool muffler gave the outfit color and would be welcome if the wind was chilly. She brushed her hair out loose, noticing how the sun turned it to copper around the edges. She added just a touch of eye shadow and lipstick and was ready.

When Bryan tapped at the door all she had to do was put on her muffler. Corrie didn't notice right away that Bryan had dressed more casually. It was at his rugged face that she looked. She looked at his cool green eyes and forgot all about clothes. He was quite simply the most gorgeous man she'd ever been out with. A man like Bryan couldn't possibly be shy.

"Nice," he said and placed a light kiss on her cheek. His voice was that seductive purr she'd heard before, and something inside her turned to mush.

It wasn't until she was getting her muffler and purse that she noticed Bryan was wearing faded jeans and a comfortable old black sweater. That he happened to look irresistible in the outfit was incidental. He hadn't gone to any pains to look good for her but the black provided a striking contrast to his blond good looks and did a superb job of showing off his broad chest. The jeans clung to his lean hips and muscled thighs revealing every nuance of the body beneath. It occurred to her that they wouldn't be dining at any very elegant candlelit restaurant in those jeans.

"Did your friend happen to mention we met her and Theo at the Old Mill last night?" Bryan asked as he held the door for Corrie.

"Yes, I had coffee with Bette this morning. Has your sister gone back to New York already?"

"She's gone up to Quebec. They're modeling fur coats. It seems they already have snow in the mountains there."

They walked along to the car. "Nice work if you can get it."

"Georgie seems to like it. It pays well, but it's the travel perks she really appreciates. It's a good way for her to see the world. She travels with the group, you know. One of the models called for her this morning. She seemed sensible."

"I bet she was beautiful, too!" Corrie exclaimed. She hadn't thought of that, that Georgie would introduce Bryan to all kinds of beautiful models.

Bryan examined Corrie as he held the door of his car for her. "You give her pretty strong competition," he said with a grin, the sun glinting on his face. "I thought we'd drive into Vermont, to the foothills of the Green Mountains, and see the scenery. Is that too far to suit you?"

When he smiled with such open admiration, Alaska didn't seem too far to suit her. "Great. Bette and Theo are going to Vermont to see the leaves today, too."

"We'll probably see half the population of Barton Falls there gawking at leaves."

"You'd think we didn't have any leaves of our own," she said, looking at the incredible wash of colors that shaded the streets.

"It's a good excuse to ask a lady out for what would otherwise be a mundane drive. Not much to do in Barton Falls on a Sunday afternoon."

There it was again—excuse. Corrie smiled encouragingly and moved a little closer to him. "You don't have to feel you need an excuse to ask me out anytime, Bryan," she said. There was an invitation in her voice.

Bryan didn't follow up the invitation. He didn't even look at her as he put the car in gear and drove off. Was he really that shy? Before long they were out of the city, heading west on Route 67 toward the Green

Mountains. The whole countryside was on fire with the raging flames of autumn colors.

"Why didn't you call me last week?" Corrie asked.

Bryan hesitated before he answered. The lady wasn't pulling any punches. Could he say it was because he didn't want to ravage her? That he had arranged to meet Helmer at the *Herald* office on purpose so he could catch a glimpse of her without asking her out? That glimpse was enough to show him he was in deep trouble. Should he tell her he'd made an excuse to leave his office on Friday so he wouldn't have to see her again, then had come rushing back early, afraid he'd missed her? He'd sound like a lunatic.

Asking her out today hadn't been a good idea, but if he had to see her—and it seemed his heart had a mind of its own in the matter—then a Sunday afternoon drive seemed fairly harmless. But for it to remain that way, Corrie would have to stop coming on to him.

"I was pretty busy," he said vaguely.

"You weren't busy last night."

"*You* were. Your friend mentioned you had a date."

Corrie smiled softly to herself. So Bette had been trying her hand at making him jealous. Good for Bette! "You didn't know that Saturday afternoon," she teased.

"It was Georgie's birthday. Since I hadn't known she was coming home, I didn't have anything planned, so I took her out. Nineteen. She's been calling herself nineteen all year. Now she's calling herself twenty." And why are you babbling like an idiot, he added silently to himself.

Corrie drew up her courage and dropped a deliberate and obvious hint. "I'm not busy next Saturday," she said.

Bryan's head turned slowly and he gazed at her. Every instinct urged him to make a date on the spot. He looked at Corrie, noticing her wide-spaced clear eyes, innocent of life. She wasn't so young in years, but experience hadn't touched her yet. "I don't know if that's such a good idea," he said stiffly.

She saw an inscrutable question in his eyes. Something in that look sent shivers up her spine. It wasn't the look of a shy man—quite the contrary.

In confusion she said, "Suit yourself."

Again he ignored her invitation. "Do you date a lot, Corrie?"

"An average amount, I guess."

"Ever had a serious relationship? An affair, I mean."

The atmosphere was becoming tense. "I've never lived with anyone."

"It'd be a little inconvenient for me to live with someone in a small city like Barton Falls. The gossip mills work overtime."

She stared at him, aghast. "Good heavens, I don't want to live with you! I have a reputation to think about, too, you know."

He arched an eyebrow and grinned. "Then you better not go putting ideas in my head."

"It's news to me if going out on one date leads to living together."

"That depends on the date. Let's just stick to admiring the leaves and forget about admiring each other, okay?"

If that wasn't a snub it was close enough to it to make Corrie's temper flare. "I don't know where you got the idea I was admiring you," she snipped.

"Your eyes said it. And in a way, you said it, too. You don't hint for a date with a man you don't like at least a little."

"As you said, that depends on the date." She stopped and decided to tell him why she'd ever become interested in him in the first place. It was a compliment to his looks, period. It didn't give him any reason to believe that she wanted to do more than be seen with him.

His eyebrow quirked up in a question. "Meaning?"

"Meaning I wanted to take you to the office party to impress my colleagues."

Bryan's eyes left the road long enough to notice the splotch of pink lighting her cheeks. "Any colleague in particular?" he asked.

"All of them, but one more than the others. A man I used to go out with."

"I see." His lips quivered uncertainly. A kid! Positively adolescent. Bryan was strangely relieved that her come-on had been so innocent. She just wanted to make her ex jealous. "You only wanted my body," he joked.

"Wrong. I wanted your body fully clothed in the most exquisite suit you own. It was childish of me. I'm sorry." As Corrie spoke, she moved a little closer to her own window and farther away from Bryan. The silence stretched between them, she took a peek and saw him laughing.

"Go on, say it," she exclaimed angrily. "I've been acting like an idiotic teenager."

Bryan reached across and drew her hand into his. "Why do people think it's immature to have feelings? It's human, not childish. I bet Methuselah's old gray head was full of jealousy occasionally. We all feel jealous at times. I must admit, I feel a twinge myself about this guy you want to impress."

His laughter had turned to a nice smile. It was the look he wore when he was with his sister. A little indulgent, definitely approving. Corrie felt better to know he understood. Funny, she hadn't thought Bryan would be so understanding.

"And by the way, I'm also flattered," he added. "If that was an invitation to your office party, I accept."

"You do?" She blinked in surprise.

"Sure, I'll act like I can't take my eyes off you, and the old boyfriend will be back in line in no time. Of course, you'll have to behave as though you're crazy about me, too. I'm looking forward to it."

"Oh, it's all over between me and the ex now. He's married to a leggy blonde."

"Then it's revenge you're after. Revenge is also human, but less commendable than jealousy."

Corrie listened thoughtfully. "I'd already decided not to bother trying to impress anyone." Not even Harry, she mused. That demon was finally put to rest. She hardly thought of Harry these days.

"Are you rescinding your offer?"

"No way."

"Then you'd better tell me the time and date."

"Two weeks from last night. Cocktails at seventhirty, dinner at eight, dance after, if you're up to it."

"I'll start training right away. And Corrie, wear your red dress, the shiny one you wore to the school reunion."

So he had noticed and remembered! "Why?"

"I'm human, too. I want to be with the most striking woman in the room."

"Unfortunately, she'll be with my ex," Corrie said.

"That doesn't sound as though you're completely over him."

"Ancient history," she insisted and changed the subject. "Look at that beautiful stand of trees, Bryan! Can we get out and walk through them?"

His smile was ingenuous. "Why not? I better start getting in shape for the dancing."

He pulled off to the side of the road and got out. Corrie noticed he was already in prime shape. You couldn't pinch half an inch anywhere on his body. He opened her door, and she stepped out into the fairyland of rampant nature.

Chapter Seven

The sun was a ball of fire in the azure sky overhead. Cottony clouds scudded along on the breeze that held the tantalizing scent of autumn. Somewhere nearby leaves were being burned. The aroma carried Corrie back in her mind to autumns in Maine when she and Rob, a childhood friend, had first raked the leaves into piles, then rolled in them like frisking animals. Then they had to rake them up again and finally, when the adults were ready, they'd be burned.

The smell was an open sesame to childhood memories. Halloween was fast approaching. Apples and pumpkin pies and costumes of witches and devils whirled in her head. Corrie could hardly stand still. She wanted to pitch herself down that hill studded with maples, all fiery red and orange, with the darker evergreens watching over them like guardians. At the bottom of the hill, a crystal clear stream gurgled by.

She used to throw rocks into the stream at home and hazard a crossing. If you fell in and got your shoes wet, that was all right too, except that you had to hide them behind the radiator and get them dry before your mom saw them. "Shoes don't grow on trees. They cost money."

She drew a nostalgic sigh. When had life got so darned complicated? Somewhere along the way the fun had gone out of it.

"Race you," Bryan challenged.

Caught between the past and present, she felt for an instant like a child again. Before she knew what Bryan meant, he had grabbed her hand and pulled her toward the top of the incline. Then he released her hand and flung himself onward at a more perilous pace. His body slanted into the wind at just the right angle. He'd done this before. Laughing, Corrie followed. The wind caught her hair and blew it all awry. It pulled at her red muffler, drawing it up behind her as she careered down the hill, shouting out loud.

Bryan reached bottom seconds before her. He put out his arms and caught her as she lost control and nearly fell. His arms closed around her, pulling her against his chest. For half a minute he just held her, savoring the warm softness of her body against his, the light herbal scent of her hair that tickled his nose. Then he pulled himself to reluctant attention and released her. Her breath came quickly, and her whole face glowed with pleasure.

"I win," he smiled.

Corrie put her head back and laughed. "That means I have to carry your books. That was the penalty when I used to do this aeons ago with Rob."

"You've been dating that long! Funny, you don't look aeons old." Ten or twelve was more like it.

"Rob wasn't exactly a date. We were only in grade two or three at the time. He always let me win." She pouted playfully.

"Aha! A spoiled child. That sounds like my sister." That was the way to think of her—as an alter ego of Georgie. "Do you want to collect chestnuts?" he tempted. "We can go home and make conkers."

Corrie gazed around at the forest. "Some naturalist. There aren't any chestnut trees here. There's an oak," she said, pointing to a tall, yellow tree. "We can collect acorns."

"And watch great oaks grow, if you have a decade or three to spare."

Bryan took her hand, and they followed a path into the woods. Through the branches, fast losing their leaves now, sun dappled the forest floor. They waded through the leaves, kicking up swirls as they went, setting loose that special aroma of an autumn woods. The pungent tang of leaves starting to decay, of pollen and moss and resin. The brightly colored branches filtered the sunlight to a golden glow that shone magically around them. When they spoke, their voices echoed as in a cathedral.

Beneath the trees, the last purple asters and goldenrod sprouted where they could find some sun. Bryan felt the seductive pull of nature and tried to break the spell. "I hope you don't suffer from hay fever," he said.

She glanced up at him and shook her head. "Spoken like a true philistine. The woods are full of beauty, and you think of hay fever."

"I sell a lot of antihistamines this time of year." But it was that other fever that began to worry him. There was no chemical cure for passion. An ounce of prevention was what was required. They were isolated in one of the most romantic spots in America. Every leaf on every tree called forth his natural instincts. A squirrel on a branch looked down and twitched his tail, chattering insolently.

"Sorry, old boy, but the neighborhood isn't going to ruin. We're just passing through," Bryan said.

"Trespassing through," Corrie added. She stopped and looked all around, smiling at the whirling leaves that fell like gigantic, colored snowflakes. "There's the oak," she said, pointing to the right. "We'll have to leave the beaten path. Are you sure you want acorns? You can't eat them, and they make lousy conkers. Not much good for making medicines either, as far as I know."

"I'll pass on the acorns."

"Let's see if we can find the stream. I can hear it gurgling. Listen."

They stood in the silence, trying to locate the source of the sound. "This way," Corrie decided. "Follow the ferns. They like wet ground."

Fallen pine needles made the ground slippery underfoot. Raspberry branches clutched at their slacks as they pushed through the underbrush to find the silver gurgling stream. Past the last stand of bushes she found it, but it was only a trickle. "Darn! It's too small to be a challenge," Corrie said. "I thought we might have a leaping contest."

"I see you're competitive. So am I. We'll have to settle for racing milkweed pod boats."

"You don't race milkweed pods. You pull them open and scatter the seeds. Don't you know anything Bryan?" She laughed. "You race daisies and dandelions, and it's too late in the season for them."

Bryan gazed softly down at her. She was making it easy to treat her like a sister. "In Barton Falls you separate the two halves and race milkweed pods," he insisted. "Fairy canoes we used to call them when we were kids. Of course, that was last year," he added with mock seriousness.

"We're not at Barton Falls. Are you sure we're even in New York State? We might be in Vermont by now, and New England is my territory."

"We didn't pass any signs saying so. If we want to see the Green Mountains, we'd better get going."

"Yes, let's go," Corrie said reluctantly with a last look around. "The Green Mountains should be beautiful today—all red and orange and gold. They must have named them in the spring."

As they stood close together, a loud clap like thunder came from the bush beyond, followed by a strange, whirring noise. Hunters! Bryan thought. He instinctively pulled Corrie into his arms and protected her with his body behind the closest tree. His heart hammered in his throat, and he was aware at the fringe of consciousness that the greater fear wasn't for himself, but for Corrie. "Don't shoot!" he shouted. "People are here!"

He heard a snickering laugh coming from the general vicinity of his chin and looked down. "This could be dangerous!" he warned. His worried frown softened to desire as he gazed into her clear gray eyes. He became minutely conscious of the feel of her in his arms and of the desire to kiss her. He'd never kissed Corrie, except in thought.

She lifted one arm and pointed to the sky, where a large grayish-brown bird beat its powerful wings in flight. "Ruffled grouse," she said. "They make that noise when they take off." Laughter lit her eyes and caused a dimple in her left cheek. He hadn't noticed that dimple before. He felt an overwhelming urge to kiss it.

"Show-off," he said in that purring voice that always sent a shiver along her spine. His eyes glittered as he went on gazing at her, lingering on the glint of copper in her tousled hair and the dappled shadows of leaves on her upturned face.

"You can let me go now," she said. "The grouse won't shoot us."

Bryan moved his arms, but only to stretch them along either side of her, caging her between the tree and his body. "Don't I get a reward for trying to protect you?" he asked. His eyes went to where the dimple had been, but it was gone. She wasn't laughing now, but she wasn't frightened, either. The glow in her eyes wasn't fear. She was excited by his closeness. It was time for that ounce of prevention. No, better make it a pound.

"Protect me from a bird?" She laughed nervously. "Gee, I hope there aren't any groundhogs around here. We'd both be in mortal peril."

As she spoke, her eyes drifted to his arms imprisoning her against the tree. All she had to do was bend her knees and she could slip out. Why didn't she?

She lifted her gaze slowly to his face as he smiled down at her. She felt an urge to run her fingers through his hair. While she looked, Bryan transferred his weight to one arm and touched her cheek with the other hand. His fingers were tantalizingly gentle.

"You have a dimple when you smile," he said softly.

"It's not a dimple. It's just a crease."

"Don't resist my compliments. You have a dimple and the longest eyelashes I've ever seen." His voice had gone beyond a purr. It was a velvet echo in her ear. Oh Lord, he was kissing her ear, and the reverberations shook her to the core.

"You should see the ones I have at home in my drawer," she said, trying to break the mood, but her voice sounded shaky.

His lips had left her ear now to nuzzle her jaw. A frisson of excitement swept through her, leaving her weak. His lips brushed softly down to her throat, while he moved the free arm behind her back to gather her against his chest. It was warm and firm and comforting. "Next you'll tell me you're wearing a wig." He cradled his face against her silky hair as he spoke.

Corrie put her hands on his chest to push him back. His other arm went around her, drawing her tightly against him. She saw the question in his eyes and mentally answered it. What's wrong with one kiss? You wanted to encourage him, didn't you? He's not a sex fiend, after all. He didn't even try to kiss you before, and you were sorry. Now, just because you're alone with him in the woods...

She lifted her face and touched his lips with hers. His lips moved, quivered a moment against hers, then firmed to hardness as she wrapped her arms around his neck. He pressed her against the tree, protecting her with one arm while the other crushed her against him, moving possessively over her back, slipping down to tighten her against his hips. She felt the solid pressure of his thighs and a pulsing throb stirred to life deep within her. It shook her to the core.

She had to open her eyes a minute to see she wasn't dreaming the whole thing. It was really Bryan kissing her, as if he meant it. Her arms tightened as she reveled briefly in the glory of it, oblivious to what it meant. He had both arms around her now, crushing her until she could hardly breathe, as if he wanted to absorb her body into his. Their thighs pressed as he held her pinioned to the tree. The quiver deep within her became a quake. This was beginning to get out of control.

She put her hand on his shoulders and pushed. His grip tightened and his lips moved hungrily. She felt a flicker of moist warmth, and suddenly he had invaded her mouth. His tongue moved languorously with sure, seductive strokes. The quiver became an explosion, and suddenly she didn't want it to stop. A soft echo of desire sounded in her throat, and her arms went around his waist, clutching desperately. The thin layer of sweater hardly lessened the intimacy. She could feel the hard strength of his chest, the lean warmth of his torso caressing hers.

For one frenzied instant it seemed the sun had fallen from the sky to consume them in its heat. Then Bryan stiffened and pulled away. I must be mad! he thought. Some big brother! Taking advantage of a kid.

He shook his head and tried to find a polite out for them both. ''You should be ashamed of yourself, Ms.

James," he joked, but his voice was unsteady. "Putting ideas in my head."

Corrie looked at him in confusion. "Funny, I had the feeling you were the one with the ideas."

"Sure, blame it on me." He laughed easier now and stepped back. "Let's go, or all the leaves will have fallen by the time we get there. It will be Barren Mountains."

He took her hand and they retraced their steps. The sun still shone. The sky was still azure and the leaves were still beautiful, but some pleasure had gone out of the day. Conversation was a little strained as they continued the trip. Corrie wanted to talk about what had happened in the woods, but Bryan was careful to avoid the subject. He talked about his work, and Corrie decided it had been just one of those things—a moment's impulse, best forgotten.

He was still fun to be with, and he was going to the office party with her. It seemed she'd have to settle for that—for the time being.

"What's new in the newspaper business?" he asked.

Corrie made an amusing story of some of the bizarre letters she received in reply to her column on the lack of commitment. It wasn't a day to talk of the tragic ones, and Bryan wasn't the man to tell about her own feelings in that area. It might sound as though she had a personal motive in telling him.

"It's odd that people will write to a perfect stranger about such intimate things," he remarked.

"Some things are best discussed with an objective stranger. People feel freer to tell the truth to someone they won't have to meet the next day. And some people don't have family or a close friend to talk to. I've had some long, fairly involved correspondence with strangers. You begin to feel, after a while, that they're your friends. I look forward to hearing what happened to some of them. It gives a real sense of satisfaction when things work out and someone writes telling me she's getting married.''

"That's the ultimate goal, is it? Marriage, and they all live happily ever after,'' he said ironically.

Corrie realized he had read between the lines. She had revealed more than she meant to. "It shows a real commitment at least. It's easy to get out of a live-in relationship—maybe too easy. Barton Falls is a conservative town. Mr. Helmer doesn't want me advising free love.''

Bryan turned to her. There was a bright, questioning look in his eyes. "I'm surprised you let someone else determine what you publish as your own beliefs.''

She stared back, unblinking. "I happen to agree with Mr. Helmer, or I wouldn't write the column.''

"When you mentioned earlier that you had your reputation to consider, I thought that was the only deterrent to living with someone.''

"No, it was an important but minor consideration.''

"I see.''

From the corner of her eye, she noticed that Bryan was deep in thought. Had he actually been considering asking her to move in with him? It was a new and alarming thought.

"I guess you can take the girl out of Maine, but you can't take Maine out of the girl,'' Bryan said musingly.

"Make that woman and you've got it about right. Oh, look at the view, Bryan!"

They were approaching the mountains. Ahead, the glorious sweep of Technicolor trees spread before them, incredible in their brightness. Bryan pulled off the road and stopped.

"Don't you sometimes wonder what the Pilgrims thought when they spent their first fall here and saw this?" she asked. "Autumn in Europe is dull by comparison."

Bryan looked a moment at the beauty of the trees, then turned to stare at Corrie. "I think I know how they felt," he said with an enigmatic smile. He felt the same way when he discovered Corrie's view on life and love. He had already suspected it, and now she had confirmed that she actually lived by that strict code. It had been a long time since he'd met an idealist. But ideals, by definition, were impractical, unobtainable, and about as enduring as this autumn splendor.

"What the poor unsuspecting souls didn't know was the bleak, frozen winter before them. Nothing like that in western Europe either," he said.

Corrie gave a tsk of disgust. "Pessimist! There's always spring to look forward to. Besides, winter isn't so bad if you know how to handle it."

"And how's that?" he asked with interest.

"With several layers of insulation. You should know that by now. Barton Falls gets pretty cold, too."

"I usually take my vacation in the winter and go south," he said. He put the car in gear and they continued their drive. Insulation—that's what he needed. Several layers of time and distance.

By seven o'clock they had had their fill of the scenery and were ready to eat. They stopped at a country inn. The air was heavy with the odors of roast beef and apple pie, nutmeg and cinnamon.

"I'm so hungry I could eat a horse," Bryan said.

"I'll have a small cow instead. The roast beef makes my mouth water."

It was a rustic place, with pine furniture and red table cloths. The walls were hung with dried corn and stalks of grain, and on the sideboard there was a centerpiece of pumpkins and various squashes.

"This takes you back to the Pilgrims, too," Bryan said.

Over a dinner of succulent roast beef, they discussed the Pilgrims—why they had come to America, how they survived, and flourished.

"It must have been a hard life, but very satisfying," Bryan said. There was a wistful echo in his voice. "A whole new world to conquer."

"There are lots of new worlds still to conquer," she pointed out. "You, especially, should know that. Your work—organic chemistry. We're only on the threshold of that."

"Yes, but at the end of a day, your muscles aren't tired from chopping wood and clearing the land. You have a headache from doing equations and fighting with suppliers for sending you the wrong ingredients. Then you go home alone," he added.

"To central heating and dinner prepared for you by a cook. You have a pretty good life, Bryan. Millions would envy you."

"No sympathy, huh?" He grinned.

"You're crying into your caviar."

"I hate caviar."

But he did actually love his work. Why had he tried to evoke her sympathy? And why hadn't she noticed his remark about going home alone? Even more importantly, why had he said it? He liked the independence of living alone. No wife to scold you if you were late. If you wanted to go to New York for the weekend, you went. If you wanted a sports car, you didn't have to worry that the kids wouldn't fit in the back. No kids to worry about, period.

Independence, he loved it. But it *was* lonesome going home to a house with only servants to greet you. "Good evening, Mr. Holmes. What time would you like dinner?" The meat was never burned. The gravy was never lumpy. Your shirts were always clean. It was boring. He looked across the table and thought how different it would be to come home to someone like Corrie. Except that marriage was forever. He was being foolish. He didn't want to stick his head in a noose.

At the next table, a couple with two children, a boy and a girl, were arguing with the boy about eating his carrots. "I don't like carrots," the boy said.

"The joys of parenthood," Bryan said in a low aside to Corrie, and laughed ironically.

"Where would we be if our parents had felt that way? I thought you were dissatisfied with your soft life. You want a challenge, you're looking at it."

"I'm hearing it," he said as the boy let out a scream.

It was perfectly obvious Bryan wasn't liking what he heard and saw. "If that's the way you feel, you shouldn't have children," she said.

"What are your views on having children?" he asked, making sure his voice was disinterested.

"Oh, I'd like a couple, I guess. A boy and a girl."

She looked to the next table, where the girl was giving her brother a lecture. She was a freckle-faced girl with blond braids. "Eat your carrots, Max. They let you see in the dark. I'm eating my carrots. I'll see in the dark tonight, and you won't."

The boy gave his sister a sulky look and ate a carrot. Bryan looked at the girl. She smiled at him. A reluctant smile eased his lips. The girl leaned aside and said to her father in a parody of grown-up manners, "Don't worry, Dad. I'll make him eat his carrots and grow up strong like you."

The love and pride on the father's face was in no way hidden by the smile he exchanged with his wife. It was a touching moment. Corrie laughed, but Bryan found himself more deeply moved. He felt a lump in his throat and a deep pang of envy for that man, surrounded by his wife and family. He was becoming soft in his old age.

"Hero worship," Corrie explained. "A lot of girls feel like that about their fathers. I know I did. One of the real joys of parenthood," she added.

Bryan played with his fork, moving his food around rather than eating it. "Eat your carrots, Bryan," she joked, "or you won't grow up big and strong."

"It's that seeing in the dark that really interests me," he said and ate his squash, as there were no carrots on his plate.

They lingered over their coffee and apple pie. "I must have eaten about ten thousand calories," Corrie said. "And night's the worst time, too. You don't burn them off as easily at night."

"You sound like Georgie."

But she was coming to remind him less of Georgie with every minute that passed. Corrie was in a class by herself. An idealist, who had every intention of living out her ideals. If he wasn't serious about Corrie, he shouldn't go on seeing her. She'd made her feelings perfectly clear. She believed in a traditional marriage, with children, and obviously that meant a man who felt the same way.

What had turned him against the idea? Was it the marriages of his friends, which were hardly like marriages at all? Or was it the women he usually went out with? If they wanted marriage eventually, they were perfectly willing to share their intimacies without it. It wouldn't be like that with Corrie. He already felt he knew her better than most of the women he'd made love with. A man in his position attracted the wrong kind of women, he decided. Or did he seek them out?

Somewhere along the way he'd thought he'd lost his belief that any other sort of woman existed. Yet he couldn't really believe it, or he wouldn't be watching over Georgie like a worried father. He certainly wouldn't approve of Georgie living the way he did. Was that the similarity he saw in his sister and Corrie James? Protective—that was the trouble. But he'd never had to protect Georgie from himself. That was a new and troublesome dimension.

He looked across the table, and she smiled at him. Every nerve in his body wanted to hire a room at this inn and carry her up to bed. He wanted to bury his face in her chestnut hair and trace the curve of her jaw with his lips. He wanted more than just to kiss her. He wanted to undress her and feel her soft femininity against him—all of it.

"Good coffee," he said.

"It'll probably keep us awake for hours."

Hours that could be spent upstairs together, in that bed. It would probably be a brass bed with a homemade quilt. The inn was quaint.

The family at the next table were leaving. "We've blown the bankroll," the wife said when the bill came in. "Tomorrow it's back to basics. Will you have your hamburg *en* casserole or *en* bun tomorrow, Bill?"

The husband put his arm around her waist and squeezed. "As long as I have it with you, it can be *en* paper plate."

Laughing, they each took one of their children by the hand and left. The little girl was clutching on to her father's hand. At the door, he lifted her into his arms. "You're squeezing my doll, Dad!" were the last words they heard from the family.

"The hero has feet of clay," Bryan mentioned, but it didn't stop that feeling that he'd like to be holding his own daughter in his arms. More and more, he was thinking he'd like that daughter to resemble Corrie James. It was a new idea for him, and he wanted to think about it before committing himself.

"Shall we go?" Corrie asked.

Darkness had fallen when they went outside. They were fifty miles from Barton Falls—an hour's drive. With leisurely, companionable conversation, the hour passed quickly. Corrie wondered if she should invite Bryan in. It was only nine-thirty.

"Would you like some coffee?" she asked.

No, I'd like you! "I have some work to do. I'd better get home. It was a . . . a nice day, Corrie."

"I had a good time. Thanks, Bryan."

She felt let down when he walked her to the front door. A nice day—was that all it was? He didn't even say he'd call her this time. She studied his brooding face. "What's the matter?" she asked.

"Matter? Nothing." But that smile was phony. "I'll call you before the party, the office party I invited myself to."

The party wasn't for two weeks. "Fine. Well, good night."

And still he went on, just looking, with a question in his eyes. "Good night, Corrie." He kissed her lightly on the forehead. His lips clung a moment, but didn't seek out her lips, and she didn't encourage him.

Corrie went upstairs alone. From Bette's door, she heard the sound of voices. Theo was still there. Why hadn't Bryan accepted her offer to come in for coffee? Corrie had a pretty good idea she'd scared him off with her talk about marriage and children. But if he was so immature that he wasn't ready for that, then there was really no point in seeing him again. She was almost sorry she'd asked him to the office party. Of course, he'd make a great impression on all her coworkers. That's all a man like Bryan was good for— making an impression. She went to the window and closed the drapes with an angry jerk.

Best to forget him, she decided, except that he refused to leave her mind. She felt the echo of that quiver up her spine when he'd held her imprisoned against the tree. Didn't that kiss mean anything? He was so right in so many ways—not only handsome but

intelligent and fun to be with. What was the matter
with everybody nowadays? Why were they so afraid of
the word marriage?

Bryan sat in his car, looking up to see what light
went on. She lived in the corner apartment on the third
floor, he decided, when that window suddenly beamed
yellow. He watched as she closed the drapes and
wished he was up there with her tonight. But tomorrow and tomorrow and all the tomorrows to come? He
slowly turned the key and drove away.

Chapter Eight

T ry to forget her. There are plenty of other women out there," Corrie wrote in answer to another of those poignant letters. It was from a man this time, complaining about a woman who wasn't ready to undertake marriage. How facile her advice sounded. She'd been trying to forget Bryan Holmes for the past week, but the image of those laughing green eyes was etched deeply in her mind. The perfect man—except for one little flaw. He was an incorrigible playboy.

But life went on, and that day Corrie had an interview with Marilyn Foster at the bank to distract her mind from Bryan. The "Interesting Women" column on Bette was almost all done. It would run first. Jan Walker from Holmes Chemical had suggested Marilyn as the subject of a column. Corrie hadn't really excepted to hear from Jan again, but she'd called to suggest lunch, and they'd gone out on Tuesday.

Corrie wondered at the time if it had been by chance or prearrangement that one of Jan's co-workers had joined them. Later Jan admitted she'd set it up.

"I was hoping to introduce Larry Hauser to you at my party," she confessed. "But when you couldn't come, I promised him I'd try to arrange a meeting. He spotted you in my office when you did my interview. He was very interested. He's new in town and lonesome. Since you mentioned you weren't seeing anyone special, I thought you two might hit it off. He's a nice fellow—a bright chemist, too."

"He seems bright. I'd be happy to go with him if he calls. Are you seeing anyone at the moment, Jan?"

"I'll be getting married at Christmas," Jan replied. "I met my husband at Holmes. He's Bryan's purchasing manager. That's the boss—Bryan Holmes."

"I've met Bryan," Corrie said, and exercised her control not to ask any questions about him.

"That figures." Jan laughed. "Bryan usually manages to meet all the attractive women in town."

It was right after that leading comment that Jan mentioned Marilyn Foster as a column subject. No more was said about Bryan Holmes and his habit of meeting all the attractive women.

Corrie was a little uncomfortable with the idea of going out with one of Bryan's employees, but Larry Hauser was good company. It was too much to expect her to ignore the whole company just because she happened to know the boss. Larry was the kind of man she'd been trying to meet for a year—the kind who wasn't afraid of a commitment. When he asked her out to dinner the next day, she accepted. It beat sitting at home, wondering if Bryan would call.

Bette was so busy since meeting Theo that she was no company at all. On the rare occasions when she was home for a night, Theo was with her. Bette was finally having her exhibition. She wanted to capitalize on Corrie's Saturday article featuring her as one of the town's prominent women.

"I'm delighted for you, Bette, but I didn't think you could afford to rent the showroom at the hotel," Corrie said when Bette told her the latest news.

"The *new* hotel," Bette added proudly. "I *couldn't* afford it. It's a vicious circle. I couldn't afford an exhibition, so no one who matters gets to see my work or buy it. I don't sell, so I can't afford an exhibition."

"How come you can afford it now? Was it Kathy's Kittens?"

"No, they're paying the rent and buying my junk food. Theo likes junk food, too. He's lending me the money. I know, I shouldn't let him, but it's only a loan. I'll pay him from my sales and he thinks I'll sell out. I've got ads in the *Herald*, and your article about me should help. I thought it was rushing it to have the exhibition this Sunday, but the hotel's pretty well booked up, and Theo thought I should strike while the iron's hot."

Theo—his name cropped up in every second sentence. "He may be right," Corrie said. "In any case, I'll be there."

"Good, bring along any friends you want. The more the merrier. Are you seeing anyone at the moment?"

Corrie told her about Larry Hauser and how she'd met him.

"Bring him to the exhibition, and Jan Walker, too. I'm afraid the place will be half-empty. We hired the ballroom. Nothing came of the Bryan thing?" Bette asked a moment later.

"Nothing serious. I'm taking him to the office party, though."

"That should make Harry Danton sit up and notice."

How childish it sounded. Corrie was ashamed of herself. She could hardly believe she'd been so childish. Spite, that's all it had been. "I don't care about that. I wish I hadn't asked Bryan."

"You really like this Larry?" Bette smiled.

"Yes, he's nice."

Nice, but he wasn't Bryan Holmes. He was a dark-haired, handsome man. He even had a sense of humor, but he didn't have green eyes flecked with gold. Corrie's heart didn't soar with pleasure when she picked up the phone and heard his voice. Larry's views on commitment or lack of it didn't interest her in any personal way. She went out with him that Saturday, and as he wanted to see her on Sunday, she invited him to Bette's exhibition.

Corrie was happy for her friend, but there was sadness, too. Bette would marry Theo. She could see it coming. Her best friend would be moving out, leaving a hole in her life. Bette had managed the miracle of finding a man who was ready to settle down. If Bette could do it, surely she could, too. The problem was, she wasn't really looking. There was Larry Hauser right under her nose, and all she could do was regret that he wasn't Bryan Holmes.

The exhibition was going to be a gala affair. The *Herald* was sending their arts and entertainment reporter. Invitations had gone out to the more prominent citizens of Barton Falls who might conceivably buy a painting. Wine and cheese were the refreshments.

"Imported wine and six kinds of cheese," Bette had told her. "Theo thought good wine was better than cheap champagne. French champagne costs an arm and two legs." These days, Theo's advice was usually followed.

Bette was wearing a long skirt, but a good short dress was fancy enough for guests. Corrie's eyes were drawn to her new red glitzy dress when she went to prepare for the exhibition. "Wear that shiny red dress you wore to the reunion." Bryan had noticed the dress and remembered. He'd remembered that she drank white wine, too. If he was paying that much attention to her, why didn't he call? If ever a person's behavior was calculated to drive her insane, that person was Bryan Holmes.

Corrie angrily pushed the red dress aside. She sorted through her closet and chose a blue wool knit with long sleeves and a full skirt. Her paisley silk scarf bordered in maroon lent it a touch of color. She arranged the scarf with a gold pin on one shoulder, gave her hair a final brushing and was ready.

When Larry arrived, Corrie asked herself if she could ever feel more than friendship for him. But no, the magical chemistry wasn't there. Larry didn't love her, either. He was lonesome, that was all. Of course it was good to have friends, too.

"A lot of the gang from work are going," he mentioned as they went down to his car.

Corrie's heart raced at the news. Maybe Bryan would be there! Bette had sent invitations to a lot of executives. "I asked Jan Walker," she said.

"She's going. I don't really know much about art. I don't care for the Picasso sort of thing."

"Bette does modern abstracts."

"I can take abstracts, as long as the artist doesn't stick a nose in one corner and an eye in the other and call it a portrait of his wife."

"Her paintings aren't like that. They're pure abstracts."

Corrie had arranged to come early and help fill the room. There were only a dozen or so people present when she and Larry arrived.

Bette came forward, ringing her hands. "It's a disaster!" she said. "I won't sell anything. I owe Theo a thousand dollars, and I'm not going to sell anything. I must have been mad. This was just an ego trip for me."

Theo seemed a changed man. He looked the same, in the same glasses and dull gray suit, but his manner was different. He was in charge and loving it. He put an assertive hand on Bette's arm and calmed her.

"It's only five after two. Nobody comes before three. Dr. Clements loves your arrangement in red and black. I think he's going to buy it."

Bette looked at him with a tremulous smile. "Really?"

"Really. See, he's back looking at it again. He thinks it's very forceful. If he doesn't know enough to buy it, I'll take it myself. It will look great over our sofa."

The "our sofa" slipped out very naturally, and Bette didn't question it. So they had been discussing marriage already. Corrie felt a premature pang of loss.

"Theo's right. It's early yet," she said. "Let's go and see the paintings before the crowd arrives, Larry. I'll help pass drinks after if you like, Bette," she called over her shoulder.

"Thanks. Say nice things out loud about my work, okay?" Bette said.

"Don't worry. I will."

Corrie went with Larry on a tour of the room. The aggressive brush strokes that had looked rough and unfinished when they were propped helter-skelter against the wall of Bette's studio had taken on a new majesty. Framed and hanging in the palatial ballroom they looked very impressive. In the first, bold slashes of black stood out angrily against shades of red. Strange to think of Bette having all that aggression locked up inside her. Would her style change now that she had Theo? This might be known as her angry divorcée period.

Corrie and Larry continued around the room, stopping to examine each piece and making the requested loud words of praise. As they made a leisurely tour, the room began to fill up.

"These look as if they were done by a man," Larry said.

Corrie frowned. "What do you mean?"

"I mean they're so... strong."

"Women can be strong, and men can be delicate. Like Watteau, or Fragonard."

"You mean the ladies in the swings with flowers and stuff?"

"Yes, all those dainty pieces were painted by men."

"I get your point, but I still don't think these are very ladylike. They're good, though. I wish I could afford one," he said, peering at the price. "If my car weren't on its last legs, I'd spring for one."

"Don't you mean last wheels?"

Corrie spotted the reporter from the *Herald* and went to talk to him. He was enthusiastic, even without any encouragement from Corrie.

"Great show. This is the lady you discovered, isn't it, Corrie? You did a column on her."

"I didn't discover her. I just recognized talent when I saw it."

"I hope you bought a couple of her paintings. It looks like a sellout."

"Really! Oh, I'm so glad for Bette. I must congratulate her."

Larry nudged her elbow. "She's talking to Jan now. Let's go and say hello."

In the general air of triumph spirits were high. Larry handed Corrie a glass of wine as they passed the table.

"I've just been introducing myself to another one of Barton Falls's interesting women." Jan smiled. "Bette and I were comparing the columns you did on us, Corrie, and we've come up with a great idea. You should do one on yourself."

"You have to be a contortionist to pat yourself on the back. I'm not even double-jointed," she joked.

Larry slid a friendly arm around her waist. "Such modesty! You have to blow your own horn, Corrie."

They had been talking for a few minutes when Jan glanced toward the door. "Here's Bryan Holmes," she said. "He mentioned he planned to come. Bryan!" She raised her hand and called him over.

Corrie looked up and felt the room spin around her. Her senses seemed preternaturally acute yet disordered. She saw mouths open in talk, but the sounds that came out were garbled. She must get control of herself. Trying to adjust her focus, she stared at the gold pendant on Jan Walker's white blouse. It was oval. The belt on Bette's long plaid skirt was crooked. You could see a part of her black sweater between the gold belt and the skirt. She should tell her.

Then she heard Bryan's voice, and it was no longer possible to avoid looking at him. He was smiling at Bette, untouched by the fact that she, Corrie James, was there.

"I recognized the name and wanted to see your work," he was saying to Bette. Then he turned to Jan. "I see you made it, Jan. Where's your fiancé?"

"Probably doing his bookkeeping to see if he can afford one of these striking paintings."

"Larry," Bryan said, nodding. That's all. Then his gaze focused on Corrie. "I should have known you'd be here, Corrie. You and Bette are neighbors, I believe?"

His voice came from far away. It sounded so cool and polite she was hurt. "Yes," is all she said. Her eyes just skimmed past his face, but in that passing glance she saw every detail. Bryan looked terrific in a tweed sports jacket and dark shirt. His hair had been brushed down to control that wayward lock. His eyes looked at her with a question.

I've got to get out of here! she thought. But it was impossible. Larry's hand was around her waist, and Bryan was talking to Larry.

"I see you're making some friends in town, Larry."

"Yes, you were right. Barton Falls is a friendly place."

"I take credit for this particular friend," Jan announced, smiling at the couple. "I arranged to introduce them. I knew they'd hit it off. They're practically inseparable."

Corrie gave an inward moan. She knew Larry was embarrassed, too. The twitching of his fingers on her waist gave it away. She risked a glance at Bryan and saw a flash of anger glint behind his lashes. Maybe it was that look that caused Larry to flinch. In any case, he let his arm drop.

Corrie decided this wasn't the moment to overcome her emotional cowardice. She had to escape. She turned with a bright smile to Bette and said, "I promised to help. I'll pass the wine now. See you later."

She picked up a tray of wine and threaded her way through the crowd. She should have suspected Bryan would be here, but he never mentioned being interested in art. He must get invited to all kinds of local dos. Did he attend them all, or had he come thinking she'd be here? Vanity! He didn't have to go to so much trouble to see her. All he had to do was lift the phone, and he hadn't done it. Yet he did seem upset that she was with Larry.

Before Corrie had served three drinks, Larry joined her. "I didn't realize you knew Bryan Holmes."

"I don't know him all that well."

Larry gave her a puzzled look. "Am I imagining things, or is he in a bad mood today? I felt scalded by that look he gave me. I thought you must be his girl or something."

So Larry had noticed it, as well. "As I said, I hardly know him."

Larry turned to look back at Bryan. Corrie found her head turning, too, against her wishes. Bryan was staring at them, and there was no denying he looked fierce. His body was rigid, and his face was hostile. As they stood mesmerized, Bryan set down his drink and began walking toward them.

Larry gave a nervous cough and said, "I think I'll just speak to Jan for a minute." He lurched off, deserting her.

Corrie decided not to acknowledge that she'd seen Bryan and continued serving the wine. She chattered inanely to the guests, trying to cover her discomfort. She was angry with herself for feeling so upset...so guilty. She felt as though she belonged to Bryan Holmes and had done something wrong to go out with Larry. It was ridiculous but it was the way he made her feel.

The minute or so it took Bryan to work his way to her side seemed endless. Her nerves were screaming when she felt the tall form hovering over her shoulder. She kept talking to the couple she'd just served, half hoping and half fearing that Bryan would leave. It seemed he always ran away just when things were getting interesting. He'd done it at her office, he'd done it at his own plant. His arm reached out and took a glass of wine.

"May I?" he asked, forcing her to look at him.

The other couple drifted off.

She looked back and felt herself being drawn into his commanding green gaze. "Of course," she said. He'd just put down a nearly full glass. Wine was an excuse to talk to her—but why?

Bryan scanned the crowd and said, "It seems to me all hands are holding a glass. Shall we just set this down somewhere and talk?" As he spoke, he took the tray and walked toward a table to set it down. Corrie didn't follow him, but waited until he returned.

"Talk about what?" she asked stiffly.

"Why, about Bette's stunning pictures, of course. That's what people talk about at an exhibition—for the first two minutes, at least."

Corrie leapt at this excuse to cover the silence. "They're lovely, aren't they?"

Bryan turned to examine them. "No, not lovely. They're exciting, dynamic. Your friend is damned good. Let's get a closer look at the red and black one. I'm thinking of buying it."

"That one seems to be a particular favorite. Theo mentioned some doctor was after it," she warned him.

They went closer to the picture, pretending they were interested, but there was a tingle of excitement in the air that had nothing to do with the exhibition. It was so strong Corrie was sure Bryan must be aware of it, too. Just as they got there, Theo stuck a Sold ticket on the white card identifying the painting. He was bustling around all that day, delighting in taking charge.

"Hello, Bryan." He smiled. "How are you doing? Is your sister here?" The casual way he asked the question showed it was only a courtesy.

"No, she's in New York," Bryan said. "That painting's sold, is it?"

"Yup, it's a beauty. Bette's good. This one is sold to Dr. Clements, the oral surgeon."

"That's too bad. I would have liked to get it."

"Too late, he beat you to it." Theo laughed and hurried off to apply another Sold sign.

Bryan stood, staring pensively at the painting, while Theo's words echoed in his ears. "Too late, he beat you to it." It seemed an omen. When you saw what you wanted, you had to move fast. Other people recognized quality, too. He had known for a week he wanted Corrie James. Wanted her for a wife. What had held him back? The uncertainty, the incredulity that he was willing to trade in his independence for a gold band.

There was no uncertainty now. His heart felt squeezed like a fist when he saw Hauser with his arm around her. He wanted to take the man outside and shake him. And he liked Larry Hauser!

"There's a very interesting painting in the far corner," Corrie said. "It's smaller than this, and the colors aren't quite so broad, but—"

Bryan looked up. "No, this was the one I wanted."

Corrie studied him. He couldn't care this much about a painting he'd only seen once. The glitter in his eyes, the rigid set of his jaws spoke of a deeper disappointment than that. He smiled ruefully and walked away, ostensibly to examine other paintings.

Bryan didn't speak for a moment. When he had recovered enough to talk he said, "Have you known Larry long?" in a conversational tone.

"No, not long."

"Love at first sight?" he asked, trying for a joking mood and failing rather miserably.

"What a romantic notion, Bryan."

"You didn't answer my question."

Why should she humor him? "No, I didn't." She turned to look at the painting. "Another one sold," she pointed out.

"About your office party..."

"I was an idiot. You don't have to tell me. If you want out..."

"I didn't say that! I thought maybe you'd prefer to take Hauser."

Corrie looked, wondering if he wanted her to let him off the hook. Was that what all this game of cat and mouse was about? He wanted to get out of it and didn't have the guts to tell her? Why should she make it easy for him?

"We're not really inseparable," she said and waited, staring at him with angry determination.

Bryan lowered his brows. When he spoke his voice was rough and impatient. "Don't play games with me, Corrie, I'm not a child. If you're seeing Larry on a regular basis... Well, there's no point in dragging this thing out, is there?"

Corrie stood her ground. If he doesn't want to see me, he's going to have to say so. "I asked you out. I'm not rescinding the offer."

"Then I guess it's up to me to do the gentlemanly thing," he said through thin lips. "Actually, I had promised Georgie I'd visit her in New York that weekend.''

Corrie had to steel herself for the blow. She felt as if she'd been kicked in the stomach by a mule. It was only her pride that carried her through. "That works out fine then. I can ask Larry to my office party. Say hello to Georgie for me.''

She walked swiftly away and just made it to the ladies' room before the hot tears spurted. For ten minutes she locked herself into the cubicle so no one would see her making a fool of herself over a man who didn't give a hoot for her. When she dried her tears and went back outside, Bryan had left.

Larry took her home soon afterward, and she invited him to the office party on Saturday night. He accepted, so that was that. Subject closed. "Try to forget him.''

Chapter Nine

On Monday evening Bette dropped in to talk about the exhibition. You could tell to look at Bette she was in love—not only with Theo, but with life. That hard, ironic look had disappeared to be replaced by a grin.

"I feel as if I'm dreaming," she said with a sigh. "I sold everything except two small paintings. The big, expensive ones all sold. I paid Theo and still have enough left to carry me for six months."

"I'm thrilled for you, Bette. And don't you have some other good news, too? I caught Theo's hint about the picture to go over your mutual sofa."

Bette's grin stretched wider. "You noticed that, huh? He hasn't asked me, but he's been talking about buying a house. He only has a one bedroom condo at the moment. Not big enough for two, he said. We went shopping one night. He wanted my advice on a sofa, since I have an artistic flair. That 'our sofa' has slipped out a couple of times.''

"You haven't known him very long," Corrie cautioned.

"How long does it take? First I liked his job and money. I admit it. I'm tired of being poor. Then I felt sorry for him when he told me about Georgie. He said he was lonesome, and she was kind to him. Kind, imagine! Then when I kissed him, Corrie, it wasn't just pity I felt.''

"*You* kissed *him*?" Corrie teased.

"He's shy. Hey, I wasn't going to let this one get away. Sometimes you have to take the initiative.''

"Yeah, and sometimes even that doesn't work," Corrie said.

"Theo and I went out to the Estaminet for dinner Sunday night to celebrate. Your friend Bryan was there with a bunch of people, including a stunning blonde.''

"Oh, really?" Corrie asked through thin lips. "He loved your black and red painting. He wanted to buy it, but it was already sold." She would *not* ask any questions. She would not lower herself to inquire if Bette recognized the blonde or how they acted together.

"It was the first one sold. I like your Larry. He's cute.''

In former days, Corrie would have discussed all the details of her love life with Bette. She would have told her that she was taking Larry to the office party and probably blown up in anger about Bryan, but she couldn't bring herself to talk about it. Not yet. The tears were too close to the surface. So she made coffee instead and urged Bette to talk about Theo.

On Tuesday morning the phone rang at work, and Corrie answered automatically.

"James here," she said curtly.

"Oh, I must have the wrong number. I'm trying to reach Corrie James. Corrie, isn't that you?" a childish voice asked. Corrie didn't recognize it immediately.

"Yes, this is Corrie James."

"Oh, hi. This is Georgie Holmes."

Corrie stared at the receiver in bewilderment. What on earth could Georgie want with her?

"I'm home for the day and I thought this might be a good time to do it."

Corrie racked her brain to see if she'd forgotten something. "Do what?" she asked.

"The interview. Didn't Fred tell you?"

"You mean Fred Helmer?" It rankled just a little that Georgie called Mr. Helmer by his first name. "He didn't say anything to me, Georgie. What's this all about?"

"I thought he would have told you. He knows I'm just home for the day. Fred wants you to interview me for your next Interesting Women column."

That column was Corrie's own project. She had thought up the idea, and she chose the subjects. Common sense told her that Georgie's job was plenty interesting, however. She should have thought of it herself.

"Mr. Helmer didn't mention it, but it sounds like a good idea. Why don't we meet for lunch?"

"Can you come to my place? I'm trying to lose three pounds, and it's impossible in a restaurant. I'm alone. Nobody would disturb us here and it'd be more private."

Corrie wouldn't really be alone. There would be servants, but as Bryan wouldn't be there, Corrie agreed. A private house was a better spot for the interview than a public restaurant. "All right. How about eleven?"

"Could you make it twelve? I'm a mess, and you'll be taking my picture."

"Twelve will be fine, Georgie."

"Great, see you then."

The phone clicked, and Corrie gave a little grimace as she replaced the receiver. Ironic that she was going to lunch at Bryan's house just when she had made a firm resolve to forget him. But business was business, it had nothing to do with Bryan. Corrie worked on the copy coming over the wire, deciding what items to include and how much space to give them, until it was time to go to the Holmeses' house. Just maybe, Bryan would drop in unexpectedly. She chided herself for the thought.

In the few weeks since her first visit to the house, lovely autumn had turned into dreary autumn. The azure skies had darkened to gray and the wind carried a bitter foretaste of winter. The trees were nearly bare. Dark skeletal branches clawed at the sky with bony twigs of fingers. The Holmes residence looked forbiddingly austere, set at the back of its long lawn.

Corrie shivered as she hurried from her car to the front door of the house.

Georgie answered the door herself. She looked like some exotic tropical bird that had forgotten to fly south. Her blond hair was dyed pink at the tips and stuck up in spikes. Her makeup was more flamboyant than usual. She had dark lines drawn around her eyes. The long purple sweater and flaming red pants didn't look as outrageous as they should have with the gold belt hanging loosely around her hips.

"Hi," Georgie said in her breathless voice. "Bleak weather, huh? Don't mind the way I look. This pink comes out of my hair. It's for some Christmas ads I'm doing. Come on in. It won't show in the black and white picture, will it? The one that will be in the paper?"

"No, it won't show," Corrie assured her and followed Georgie into the living room.

A nest of cushions, about two dozen in all, had been stacked in front of the fireplace. "I thought you could shoot me here," Georgie suggested. "It's a nice fireplace, don't you think? A real Adams my grandfather had brought over in pieces from a house in England. Let's do the picture first, before my hair starts to wilt."

Georgie assumed half a dozen professional poses while Corrie clicked away. When the photo session was over, Georgie led Corrie to the dining room at once. The table looked ready for a banquet. It was laid with white linen and china and silverware. There was even a low bowl of baby roses in the center. Should she compliment Georgie, tell her she shouldn't have gone to so much trouble? Or did the Holmes eat like this every day? She didn't want to sound like a hick.

"This looks lovely," she said blandly.

"Thanks," Georgie smiled. "I bought the flowers myself."

Corrie was touched at the shy admission. "You shouldn't have gone to all this bother."

"Oh, I was glad to do it. I'm sorry to rush you, but I have to be in New York this afternoon," Georgie explained. "I'd like to leave by one, so maybe we can eat while you ask me questions. Oh, by the way, do you want wine? It will have to be red."

Georgie's eating certainly didn't interfere with her talk. She only nibbled at a salad and about an ounce of some white fish that didn't even have a sauce. She had ordered a better meal for Corrie.

"Almost everybody likes steak, so I figured that was safe. It's medium rare," Georgie explained. "Bryan's real fussy about his steak. We get it from a butcher who supplies restaurants. Bryan says they have the best cuts."

Corrie smiled politely, ignoring any mention of Bryan, and said the steak was fine. She set her notebook beside her plate and asked all the usual questions. When did you decide you wanted to be a model? How did you prepare yourself? Are you happy with the job? What are the pros and cons? What are your plans for the future?

"I didn't exactly decide. I wanted to join the aerospace program and do something meaningful, but I wasn't very good at math and physics. Bryan wanted me to work for him. I was taking a stenographer's course when a local department store asked me to model for them. Clothes can be meaningful, too, don't you think? I mean they're important to women. You can get a lot of psychic satisfaction out of looking good."

Georgie liked talking about herself. The problem wouldn't be to fill the column, but to winnow out the wheat from the chaff.

"Try this salad dressing," Georgie urged between questions. "Bryan invented it himself. It's olive oil and lemon juice and some herbs and things. I'm not sure what all. I can't have it because of the olive oil. Zits," she explained.

Corrie drizzled a very small amount of dressing on her salad. "I usually use French dressing," she mentioned as it avoided commenting on Bryan.

"We have French! I'll get you some," Georgie exclaimed and jumped up.

"No! Please, it doesn't matter. This is fine."

"I don't want to spoil your meal." Georgie was certainly a thoughtful hostess. She looked chagrined.

Actually Corrie hardly tasted the food. She was on edge, wondering if the front door would open and Bryan would walk in. "What are your future plans?" she asked in a businesslike manner.

"I want to do all the fashion magazine covers and then do ads on TV, then become an actress. I'm taking acting lessons in New York now. My instructor says I have great stage presence. I look better on film," she explained. "I'll probably be a better comedienne than tragic actress. Wouldn't you know it? And I'd just love to play Camille. And that's about all," Georgie said.

Her plate was empty, and she picked up her coffee cup. "Black, no sugar," she said. "That's one con for the job—you're always hungry. Bryan makes me take all kinds of vitamins so I won't die of malnutrition. No dessert for me, but we have fresh fruit and cheese, or some chocolate cake with about ten hundred calories per slice. It's really terrific. Do you want ice cream on it?"

"I'll pass, thanks. I don't usually eat a very heavy lunch."

"Oh, I had Cook make it especially. But I know what you mean about lunch. You feel fat and gross all afternoon if you eat dessert. I should have asked you for dinner."

"But you won't be here, will you?" Corrie reminded her.

"No, I'm leaving at one. Oh well, I tried to make it a nice lunch," she said in a defensive tone.

"It was lovely. You really shouldn't have gone to so much trouble."

Corrie thought this lunch was probably the first time Georgie had arranged an entertainment by herself. She seemed so edgy and determined to please. Georgie smiled at the compliment and asked, "How do *you* like your job, Corrie?"

"I like it."

Georgie sipped her coffee slowly. "One con I don't want you to mention in the article is Bryan," she said.

"Your brother doesn't approve?"

"No, it's not that. It's just that I'm not here to keep an eye on him since I've been working out of New York. I thought he seemed sort of depressed when I got home this time. I guess he must have broken up with some woman or something. He won't talk to me about it." She looked a question across the table.

Corrie felt uncomfortable with this topic. If she was the woman under discussion, Bryan had no reason to be depressed. He was the one who broke their date. "As you said, I won't put anything like that in the column. It's about you, not your brother."

"We've become very close since Dad died. Bryan even comes to New York to visit me, and he's very busy, you know. I wish he'd get married," she said and gazed into her cup. "It would be good for him."

"Perhaps he's not ready for marriage."

"I think he is. He just doesn't know it. Oh well, some woman will come along and make him realize it."

For no particular reason, Corrie thought of Bette and Theo. When it happened for Bryan, it would probably happen like that—a flash romance, a wedding. The same way it had happened for Harry Danton and his new bride. Why couldn't it have happened between her and Bryan? What was the missing ingredient? The flash had hit her. It just hadn't been transmitted to Bryan.

"Theo will probably be marrying soon," Corrie said. It was easier than talking about Bryan.

"I'm glad. I'm all for marriage myself. I want to have three children eventually. Are you going with anyone, Corrie?"

"No." Georgie gave her a sharp look. "No one I'm serious about. I date, of course."

"But there's no one special?" Georgie persisted.

"I'm the one who's supposed to be asking questions. Do you have a serious boyfriend?"

"My career comes first. I have to work all odd hours and travel quite a bit. Is that why you aren't serious about any special man, either? Your career, I mean?"

"No, my job is more regular. It wouldn't interfere with marriage." Corrie looked at her watch. "I better be going."

"Not yet!" Georgie exclaimed. "I—I want to show you the fur jacket I got in Canada. It's gorgeous. I feel so pampered when I put it on, but the photographer said I should try to look savage, like a she-wolf."

"I think he chose the wrong model," Corrie laughed.

Georgie ran upstairs and while she was gone, Corrie put away her notebook and got her coat. She was waiting in the front hall when Georgie came down wearing the jacket. It was a beautiful long-haired silver coat. "It's warm as toast," Georgie said. "Want to try it on?"

There was a sound at the door. Georgie looked expectantly toward it. It opened, and Bryan Holmes stepped in. He looked questioningly at Corrie. The wind had whipped his hair askew and turned his cheeks ruddy. With the jacket of his trench coat turned up around his neck, he looked maddeningly attractive. His eyes held hers a moment.

At the first sight of him, Corrie's insides began to shake with nervousness. She had never felt so foolish in her life. After the quarrel with Bryan, it looked like chasing him to be here, right at his house. He wouldn't know Fred Helmer had arranged for the interview. A quick escape seemed the best course, but first she'd let Bryan know she hadn't come here hoping to see him.

"Hello, Bryan," she said, managing to make it sound casual. "Surprise! You didn't expect to see me again so soon." She busied herself buttoning her coat, but she noticed the angry frown that Bryan directed at his sister. What's she doing here? it suggested.

When he spoke he had subdued his anger. "Hello, Corrie. Don't rush off on my account."

That she should do anything on his account was an idea that had to be put to rest immediately. "I was just leaving. Mr. Helmer wanted me to interview your interesting sister—for my column, you know."

Bryan cast a look at his sister. "Oh really? Don't make it too flattering. Her head's big enough already. Or is that funny looking stuff hair?" he joked, looking at his sister's pink-tipped spikes.

Corrie noticed that Bryan wasn't aware of the interview. He didn't know she'd be here and he hadn't come to see her. Where had that foolish hope come from?

Georgie gave him a condescending look. "You're completely out of it, Bryan. Everybody's wearing colored tips in the city."

"I have to fly. This will be in Saturday's paper, Georgie," Corrie said. "I'll send you a copy of the article if you like."

"You don't have to do that. I have the *Herald* delivered in New York. Thanks, Corrie."

"You're welcome. Bye." She started for the door, her emotions a riot of confusion. She really should say goodbye to Bryan, too. He leapt into action to open the door for her.

"Do you have to leave this minute?" he asked with his hand immobile on the knob, not turning it.

Corrie found herself staring at a closed door, dreading to lift her eyes and look at Bryan. Yet she couldn't go on staring at the doorknob forever. She steeled herself to indifference and raised her eyes. Bryan gazed at her uncertainly. She had never seen him look so unsure of himself. He was about to say something when Georgie spoke up from the stairway.

"There's lots of coffee left. Why don't we all have a coffee? I can spare ten minutes."

Some instinct that refused to die wanted to escape that offer. Corrie glanced quickly from sister to brother. Bryan was glaring at Georgie, his lips clenched in a grim line. He was furious at her suggestion.

"I'm late already. I have to dash. Thanks for the interview and lunch, Georgie. Goodbye, Bryan," Corrie said briskly, not risking another look at him. She pulled the door open herself and escaped into the dull, gray day.

She thought she heard the echo of a rather surprised "So long," as she hurried down the stairs. Her face was pink with embarrassment and confusion when she got out of the cold into her car.

Idiot, she silently scolded herself. You acted as though he were a criminal, running as if your life depended on it. You should have strolled out casually. It would have looked more natural. Now he knows how uncomfortable you were. And why should you have been ill at ease if you didn't care? Why did he look ready to crown his sister for asking you to stay for another cup of coffee?

Corrie's evening wasn't a great success, either, but at least it wasn't nerve-racking. It consisted of an Italian dinner with Larry and a tour of the car dealers after.

"Something to match my new status at Holmes Chemical," he said grandly. "I've been put in charge of my own project. Project leader! That's pretty good for a guy who's only been with the company since the spring."

Corrie had already congratulated him twice since he'd made the announcement, but she congratulated him again. "You must be intelligent, or Bryan wouldn't have promoted you."

"I was kind of nervous when he called me into his office. After the art exhibit, remember? I thought he was going to ask me about that. I remember the way he looked at me."

Corrie remembered it, too, but she'd obviously misinterpreted that look. Bryan didn't bear Larry any grudge, or he wouldn't have promoted him so soon afterward.

They went to three dealers, then returned to the first one to buy the car. "It will be ready for our big date Saturday night," Larry told her. "I'll drive you to your office party in style. And by the way, what do I wear?"

"Just a suit or blazer. It isn't formal."

"What are you wearing?" he asked.

"A red dress," she said in a strangely choked voice. "And don't buy flowers, Larry. No one will be wearing a corsage."

She'd been wearing Theo's hideous pink rose corsage the first night she met Bryan when he had revealed his philosophy against marriage.

Harry hadn't believed in marriage either—until he met Rhonda. Georgie thought Bryan was lonesome. Had he met his Rhonda, the stunning blonde Bette saw him with Monday night at the Estaminet? Bette said something about a group, so maybe the stunning blonde was one of Georgie's model friends. What difference did it make to her anyway?

Corrie shook away these ragged tatters of memory and put her car into gear. Life goes on. Go to the office, write the Interesting Women column, hit Mr. Helmer up for some juicier work, perhaps the pending teachers' strike. More than half the teachers were women. The strike would affect the mothers, too, especially the working mothers. Interviews with some of the teachers and parents would be interesting.

It was time she got on with her career, since that seemed to be all she had in her life. Then she thought of Larry. He was beginning to get some ideas beyond friendship. It was bound to happen if she went on seeing him so often. She wouldn't go out with him again until the party Saturday night. And after that she'd back off.

When Larry called on Wednesday, she told him she was busy. She stayed home and cleaned out her closet. Twice she went to Bette's door. The first time she heard the low murmur of private conversation and went back to her own rooms. When she heard Bette's door close, she thought maybe Theo was leaving early. She looked out and saw Bette going toward the elevator with Theo. Two by two, male and female, like the animals in the ark. That was the way people went in the world, the way they were meant to go.

Her heart felt so heavy it actually ached. By Thursday evening Corrie was so lonesome and depressed she decided to barge in on Bette and Theo. She'd just stay half an hour. She was surprised when Theo answered the door. He had an apron tied around his waist and looked distracted.

"Corrie! Come on in. Bette's not here. I was just going to ask you to help me. How do you make whipped cream? The real kind, I mean, not the one that comes out of a spray can."

"Whipped cream?" Corrie asked, blinking in surprise. "Theo," she said, laughing, "what's going on here?"

"I'm making dinner for Bette. This is a kind of special night," he added, smiling.

"Oh? A birthday?" She knew it wasn't Bette's birthday, but hoped Theo might explain the cause of the celebration.

As he showed her into the apartment, she knew something special was afoot. Theo had bought flowers. There was a bottle of champagne in a bucket of ice. The aroma of Italian spices and hot bread hovered in the air.

Theo drew a blue velvet ring box out of his pocket and flipped it open. A diamond ring fashioned like a flower sparkled in its nest of white satin.

"I'm going to pop the question," he said. "Bette's gone to New York to visit the galleries, trying to get one of them to show her work. If she gets turned down, maybe this will cheer her," he said, smiling softly. "And if she gets accepted, then it will be a double celebration."

"Either way, she can't lose. I'm thrilled to death, Theo. Good luck. Now about that whipped cream—"

"It's for the pumpkin pie. I bought the pie, but I made the spaghetti sauce myself. Will you try it? I think maybe it needs more garlic."

Theo fluttered around the kitchen, as nervous as a mother hen. It was touching to see how much he cared. "I want her to see that I can pitch in and help with the cooking and housework," he explained. "Bette's not exactly the domestic type. The artistic temperament," he explained with a touch of proprietarial condescension.

The undomestic Bette didn't own a whipper. Corrie went to her apartment and brought hers over. She made the whipped cream. When it was done she put it in the fridge.

"You might have to give it another whip just before you serve it," she explained.

"Thanks, Corrie. I want everything to be perfect tonight. Wish me luck."

"All the luck in the world. You're getting a real jewel, Theo."

He hung his head like a shy boy. "Better than I deserve or ever thought I'd get. In a way, I owe it all to you, Corrie. You introduced us. I know Bette will want you to be the bridesmaid."

"I already have a dress. I was my cousin's bridesmaid last year."

"Always a bridesmaid, huh?" He laughed lightly.

The old cliché, spoken thoughtlessly, stayed with Corrie to bother her when she left. Always a bridesmaid, and the unspoken corollary—never a bride. She heard Bette arrive, heard one gasp of surprise, then the door closed. The visit hadn't cheered her at all. It had only sunk her deeper in depression to know Bette would be leaving. They'd still be friends, but it wouldn't be the same once Bette was married.

Across the hall, Theo was asking Bette to marry him. He was giving her the ring, that symbol of eternal love. He, a busy orthodontist, had taken time to personally cook her up a dinner. He wanted everything to be perfect. Bette was astute; she'd recognized in the paunchy man who made a fool of himself over Georgie the man Theo could be. She'd set to work to free him from the past insecurities of his unpopularity. Love had worked the miracle.

Why couldn't it teach her how to free Bryan from his fear of marriage? That was what made men into playboys. A fear of marriage, or a feeling that women weren't worth it. Dr. Bankes had explained how men who behaved like playboys often really despised women. That was why they didn't treat them with respect. But Bryan didn't seem to despise women.

Early Friday morning Bette dropped in to show off her diamond and announce the gallery had taken her on. "It was the best day of my life, Corrie. I got my man and I got a gallery to exhibit my art, in one day. Life can only go downhill from here."

"Don't go looking for trouble." Corrie laughed.

"Trouble? Who's afraid of a little trouble? I couldn't bear to live at this elevated stratosphere. I'd suffocate."

"Go boast to somebody else. I've got to get to work," Corrie said. "We'll talk tonight, if Theo can spare you."

"I'm going to go shopping for a wedding dress," Bette replied and waltzed, laughing, back to her apartment.

Later that day Larry called Corrie at work. She'd tell him she already had a date that night. That would give him the idea she wasn't seriously interested in him. "Corrie, about Saturday," he said.

She was relieved to hear it wasn't tonight he wanted to talk about. "Why don't you pick me up around seven, Larry?"

"That's just the thing. I can't."

"That's all right. I'll pick you up. Is there some trouble with the new car?"

"The car's fine. I have to go to Chicago to work on my project."

"On a Saturday?"

"Bryan put me in charge to straighten it out. We're behind schedule, and there's a penalty clause, so it's a rush-rush affair. I'm leaving today. The lab in Chicago has agreed to work Saturday. With luck, I'll be back the middle of next week. I'm sorry. I know your office party is a big deal. I can get you a date if you like."

"No, that's all right. I'll invite someone else."

"It's kind of short notice."

"In a pinch, I can go alone—for the cocktails and dinner anyway. I can come home before the dance starts."

"Why don't you let me ask someone? There are half a dozen guys here that'd love to go with you."

"No, really. It's fine, Larry. I'll let you go now. Bye."

Corrie felt only a vague wisp of relief when she hung up the phone. She'd been dreading that last date with Larry. There was nothing wrong with him, but the strain of trying to be good company when all she wanted was to bury herself in mud was beginning to tell. She'd go alone and leave early. Nothing wrong with that. She didn't care what Harry or any of the others thought. What was wrong with not having a date? Her date had to go out of town on business, that's all.

Going alone would establish her as her own woman. She didn't need a man's arm to hang on to. It was an office party, and she was one of the workers at the office. She began to like the idea and didn't even bother canvasing the possible men she might have asked.

On Saturday she did her usual chores and managed to work in a trip to the hairdresser in the afternoon. She met Jan Walker there. It was a good feeling to recognize people everywhere she went. That was one plus of her job, she met lots of people.

"Corrie! I was just reading your column," Jan smiled. "That Georgie Holmes is something, isn't she? So cute."

"Yes, and she has a very interesting job."

"Larry's been telling me about his dates with you. He was sorry he had to leave you in the lurch tonight. An office party, too. But I'm sure you won't have any trouble finding a stand-in."

"I'm going alone."

"Oh?" Jan gave her a quizzical look. "I could probably round up someone if..."

"No, thanks," Corrie said firmly. "I decided I wanted to go alone."

Of course Jan didn't believe her. You could see the disbelief in her eyes. The hairdresser called Jan to begin work on her and Corrie waited her turn. She flipped through the *Herald* as she sat. There was a small picture of her and her name on the Dear Corrie column. Her name without picture was on the Interesting Women column. She'd written an article on the history of Halloween and edited some of the other stories in the people section. She was gaining experience and feeling her confidence.

All this buoyed her spirits until she began to get dressed for the party. When she stood looking at the glitzy red dress, she knew just being a competent writer wasn't enough. She was dreading to go alone, not because of Harry or anyone else pitying her, but because she was alone.

She felt like half a woman. Where was the non-working half of her life? She needed someone to share her work and triumphs with. No matter how successful she eventually became at work, she'd always feel this incompleteness until she met the special some-one.

Bryan just hadn't worked out. A dull pain settled in the pit of her stomach. She wanted to crawl into bed and pull the blanket over her head. She was looking with interest at the bed when the phone rang.

Larry? Was it possible he'd managed to get back for the party? She hurried into the living room.

"Hello."

"Corrie, it's Bryan."

Bryan! She tried to speak and found herself bereft of words. What could he possibly be calling for? "Are you there?" he asked.

"Yes."

"It just occurred to me I had sent your boyfriend off to Chicago and this is the weekend of that office party, isn't it?"

"Yes." Her heart began to rev up. It pulsed irregularly like an engine badly in need of a tune-up. It couldn't be...

"It struck me that the least I could do was to offer to fill in for him, if you haven't made other arrangements."

So that was it. Just acting the perfect gentleman. His voice even sounded uncertain. "That's all right. Thanks anyway, Bryan."

"You have a date then?" he asked.

It was hard to tell his mood when all she had to go on was a disembodied voice, but he sounded a little disappointed.

"No, I'm going alone."

"I'd be happy to go with you. I'm free tonight. Seems a shame to waste that other ticket," he tempted.

Corrie's eyes went to the red dress hanging on her closet door. It seemed like fate giving her another chance. Sometimes romance blossomed in a flash. Maybe the flash would occur tonight.

"If you're sure you want to," she said. A hopeful smile trembled on her lips.

"I want to. I'll be there in about two shakes." His mood was easier to read now. It sounded wonderfully eager. "You're wearing the red dress?"

"I can, if you like."

"Make that one shake. Bye."

Corrie hung up the phone and picked up the red dress.

Chapter Ten

To be jealous is human. Not to enjoy retaliation would no doubt be divine. Corrie admitted she was only human. Stepping into the room at the hotel on Bryan Holmes's arm was one of life's small triumphs. The women were all green with envy. Any female over fifteen years of age could read the silent question in their eyes: Where did she nab *him*? The men looked first at Bryan with a measuring eye, then studied Corrie with a new interest.

Fred Helmer, guarding the door to welcome each new arrival, made a big fuss over Bryan. Corrie was thankful that her boss remembered her name and used it. He even called her Corrie when she'd always been "Miss James" before. There was a new air of friendliness in Mr. Helmer.

"Yes sir, Corrie is a very talented writer. We have big things in mind for her."

"Corrie told me on the way over here that she's interested in doing a story on the teachers' strike," Bryan mentioned. "From the point of view of the teachers and parents, and the problems it presents to them."

"And, of course, the students," Corrie added.

"A marvelous idea! The human interest element. No one could do it better," Mr. Helmer beamed. "Drop into my office on Monday, Corrie, and we'll discuss it."

So it was true. It wasn't just what you knew, but who you knew. She'd got this far on her own talent and hard work. If knowing Bryan opened the door a little wider, she'd sure slip in. And once she was in, she'd write the best darned story Fred Helmer had ever read.

"I'll be there, Mr. Helmer."

They passed on through the room, where people stood in groups, talking. From the corner of her eye, Corrie saw Harry Danton and Rhonda. They made a striking couple. Harry's rugged dark complexion was the perfect foil for the languorous, blond Rhonda whose black dress dipped daringly low in front and clung to every inch of her curvaceous body. Corrie noticed that they were staring at her and Bryan. She gave them a brightly disinterested smile, and with her hand resting possessively on Bryan's arm, advanced.

"Harry... Rhonda, nice to see you," she said and introduced Bryan to them.

Both husband and wife were smilingly friendly, perhaps a little more than friendly on Rhonda's part. Harry either didn't care or was so used to his wife drooling over men that he didn't object. How had she ever thought she was in love with Harry Danton? Oh sure, his football player's shoulders filled his jacket to perfection. His rugged face still had some charm, but it paled to insignificance beside Bryan. Bryan did a superb job of being friendly with Rhonda without encouraging her.

The men talked for a few minutes about football. Corrie realized sports was the only subject Harry could discuss with any authority. How many hours had she spent pretending she was interested in touchdowns and tackles and field goals? She saw the dull, glazed look that soon settled on Rhonda's face and pitied her. Pity was about the last emotion she had ever expected to feel for Harry's wife.

When she and Bryan walked on to the next group, Bryan leaned his head close to hers and asked, "Which is the ex I have to impress with my devotion? I want to be suitably loving." As he spoke, he slid an arm around her waist. The intimate gesture sent a thrill rushing through her.

If she told him he'd already impressed the ex, he'd move his arm. She liked the feel of it there, and not just to impress her colleagues, either. "See if you can guess," she smiled and went on to show him off to the others.

She admired that Bryan was mentally equipped to handle any of the various interests that made up a newspaper. He talked politics with the wire editor, municipal doings with the local editor, finance and entertainment and even the arts with the proper people in charge of each department.

"Where did you find the dream boat?" Mr. Helmer's secretary whispered in Corrie's ear. "Was it when you did the column on Georgie Holmes?"

"I knew Bryan before that," she answered casually.

Corrie definitely had her little moment of glory. Around dinner time it began to taste like gall. Bryan did a superb job of pretending he was crazy about her, but it was only an act. For the next few weeks at work everyone would be teasing her about him, and it would soon be clear she'd lost another man. This had been a terrible mistake because Bryan was definitely not interested. He'd made that clear as soon as he picked her up at the apartment for the date.

"Very nice," he said, running an assessing look from her head to toes. "That outfit should be enough to set your ex on his ear. You didn't need me."

He looked so handsome she wanted to pitch herself into his arms and seduce him on the spot. His blond hair had been wet to make it behave. The water made it gleam like bronze metal. His dark business suit was just right, the men wouldn't be wearing formal evening wear. A sparkling white shirt and discreetly patterned tie raised the suit a notch above day wear. He was freshly shaved, with a light, lingering woodsy scent hovering around him.

His attitude, she decided, was just right, too. That light touch served to quell her nervous embarrassment. His first speech made clear why he was here. He was just doing her a favor because he'd had to send Larry out of town on this special night. No strings attached.

"I didn't say I did need you. I planned to go alone when Larry couldn't come," she reminded him. She regretted the snippy reply as soon as it was out. It sounded so ungrateful.

Bryan shook his head, undismayed. "You women are becoming too independent. Next thing we know you'll be shaving your faces and calling yourselves Mr."

"That's about all that's left," she agreed. "We're already wearing trousers and joining the army and changing our own tires."

He gave her a laughing look. "There's still one area you haven't breached. Women make poor husbands."

She felt an oozing heat invade her body at the images that remark caused. It seemed a good time to hand him her coat. "Here, you can help me with this."

Bryan kept up the charade of being in love with her all through dinner. It was unfortunate that Harry and Rhonda sat across the table from them. What spiteful person had arranged that? Maybe it was somebody's idea of a joke, but if so, it backfired. Bryan ignored Rhonda's long, inviting looks. He talked to Corrie about their trip to the Green Mountains to see the leaves and about the exhibition, making it sound as though they'd been dating steadily for weeks.

"The night we were at the Tampico," and "When we drove to Vermont," and such misleading phrases fell easily from his lips. What was more disconcerting was the secret smile. "That will show him," it said to her, but to the others it carried a different message.

The louder he talked, the quieter Corrie became. As the dessert was being served, Bryan leaned over and said, "Am I wasting my time? I seem to be the only one of us who's wallowing in love. Is the ex not at this table?"

"He's here," she replied, but her mind grabbed on to that "wallowing in love," not pretending to be in love, but wallowing in it. Of course "wallowing" was obviously a joke. She was grasping at straws.

Bryan began a slow study of the men at the table. Old Bill Snell from the printing office and his wife, two older married couples, Harry and Rhonda, and themselves. After he made the tour, his eyes returned to Harry. It had to be him. So that's the kind of man she likes. A jock. Handsome, but . . .

Larry Hauser was better. Not quite as handsome, but more salt in the bread pan. He was a bright lad, yet she'd told Georgie she wasn't really interested in Larry, so maybe he had a chance if he did it right this time. Marriage, kids, the whole thing. Bryan's independence had become a burden he wanted to lay down. It was just another word for immaturity. Another word for lonesomeness. He was ready to tackle adulthood and he wanted to tackle it with this woman. He wanted to go to bed at night with his arms holding her close and wake up in the morning with her by his side, her expression soft with sleep and love.

He wanted her to bear his children. He wanted to feel their daughter clutch his hand and call him Dad. He wanted a son to raise, hopefully to fill his shoes at the company one day, but if the boy wanted to do something else, that was all right, too. A smile pulled at his lips. Maybe his daughter would be the one to take over the company. That'd please Corrie.

He shook himself to attention. Corrie was frowning at him. "Struck speechless at my taste, I see," she said. "You must admit he's handsome at least."

She was looking at the jock. "Well built, too," he said and couldn't remember what she was talking about. Her ex—of course! Then it *was* the football player. A piercing sting of jealousy stabbed him. "It must have been a delayed college crush. And you a Vassar grad!"

"I didn't go to Vassar," she said, looking to see if he was surprised. His only expression was impatience. "I went to a state college."

"Wherever. I understand all you coeds lusted after the football players."

"I didn't," she retaliated swiftly. "I went with the head of the debating society. We worked together on the college newspaper."

"I said a delayed college crush. You didn't give your hormones free rein at college. Then they caught up with you later in life."

A musing expression settled on her face. The man was a mind reader. That must be exactly what it was, a delayed crush on a football star. She was mortified by this unsuspected streak of immaturity in herself. "I suppose you're right," she admitted.

That incensed him, too. A working woman didn't go out with a man like Harry Danton for long without ending up in his bed. A glint of fury flashed in his eyes. "Was he as good as you hoped? Did the hormones get a good workout?"

Corrie was stunned by his tone. What had happened to his impression of a lover? He looked ready to crown somebody, possibly her. She was saved from replying by the arrival of dessert.

"A charlotte russe! How grand of Mr. Helmer. He really went all out. Last year we only had sundaes."

Bryan's hand below the tablecloth grabbed hers and squeezed. "You didn't answer my question," he growled.

She smiled demurely, but her voice was menacing. "I didn't want to be rude in company, so I decided to ignore it."

He read the challenge in her eyes. "Very well, I'll postpone the question—for now."

She withdrew her fingers and smiled provocatively. "That might be a good idea, Bryan. You wouldn't want me asking about how much exercise your hormones have had all these years, now would you?"

He met her gaze steadily. "They haven't had any since I met you, except the exercise of futility."

"Oh, really? I thought the blonde you were with at the Estaminet the other night might have given them a bit of a workout."

He looked bewildered. "Have you been spying on me?"

"Don't flatter yourself. My neighbor happened to see you and mentioned it."

"I was with my cousins from Milwaukee."

"Kissing cousin, was she?"

She was jealous, and the knowledge cheered Bryan immeasurably. "I'd be a fool to try anything like that.

Her husband makes your ex look like a ninety-nine-pound weakling.''

Bette had said Bryan was with ''a party,'' although she hadn't mentioned anyone but the blonde. It could be true.

Corrie allowed her eyes to settle admiringly on Harry Danton's shoulders. ''It must have been a big table.''

He felt like a jealous schoolboy, even while his maturer self told him she was trying to make him jealous. And why should she do that unless . . .

The waitress was pouring coffee. The charlotte russe had magically disappeared from Corrie's plate. How could she eat at a time like this? Bryan picked up his fork and began pushing the food around while planning.

''I'm sorry I had to send Larry out of town this weekend,'' he said.

She snatched at the peace offering. ''That's all right. He was probably delighted to get a chance to try out his new car on the trip. And, of course, his promotion was good news. He's delighted to be a project leader.''

After Georgie's assurance that there was nothing between Corrie and Larry, it came as an unpleasant shock that Corrie knew so much about Larry's life.

''Is it serious between you two?'' he asked.

''I've only known him a couple of weeks,'' she hedged.

Another question she chose not to answer—yet. But before she got into her apartment that night, she'd answer all his questions.

Corrie felt her nerves tingle at the determined look in Bryan's eyes. Why was he looking at her like that? It was a complicated look, made up of anger and determination and some less aggressive emotion. What it was not was the laughing eye of a man playing a role in a charade.

She was relieved when the speeches began, as it gave her time to think about things. Bryan was behaving very strangely. At times he sounded almost jealous, which was patently ridiculous. He'd had every opportunity to get closer to her and had rejected every one. Was it plain old masculine ego at work, a purely animal reaction to competition, like a couple of rutting rams banging their skulls together? She'd seen that sort of senseless machismo at work before.

Corrie felt a hand on her arm and looked down to see Bryan's fingers gently massaging her arm. He had lovely hands, long fingered, tanned, with a college ring on his right hand. She peered curiously at him. He darted his eyes toward Harry and winked at her, giving her arm a possessive little squeeze. More playacting. She smiled and withdrew her arm, using the pretext of taking a sip of coffee. When she set the cup down, he took her hand and held it lightly in his, on top of the table so Harry could see.

Bryan held her hand until the speeches were over, and she had to either let him or make an issue of it in public. She let him continue, but didn't return any pressure. As soon as the speeches were over and a polite applause rendered, people began moving toward the dance hall. Other years she'd had the first dance with her date, then mixed with other partners. She supposed she'd have to dance with Harry and dreaded it.

There weren't many people as young as Corrie at the party. The musical entertainment chosen was an old-fashioned orchestra with more saxophones and trumpets and clarinets than guitars.

"Is that a fox-trot or a waltz?" Bryan asked, laughing.

"I think it's called jazz," she said uncertainly and went into his arms.

"Wrong, child. I recognize it now. My dad used to call it swing."

Whatever it was, it was good for dancing together. Bryan held her securely locked against him. She was conscious of the body beneath that severe dark suit. She'd never seen it unclothed, but she knew the kind of a body it would be. It would be muscled and tanned, with a patch of hair on his chest. She wondered what color his body hair would be. Probably black. He had striking black eyebrows and lashes.

As they danced, his arms tightened imperceptibly around her until she was crushed against him. Her chin rested against his shoulder, and a whiff of that woodsy scent wafted past her nostrils. His thighs brushed intimately against hers, and a heat began burgeoning inside her. Bryan didn't say anything, and she was bereft of words. She wanted it to be like this between them, but for real—not a charade. For the entire length of the dance, they didn't talk. When it was over, Mr. Helmer walked toward them.

"Corrie, may I have the pleasure of the next one?" he asked. His wife smiled hopefully at Bryan.

They exchanged partners. Mr. Helmer was extremely inquisitive on the subject of her relationship with Bryan Holmes. Corrie politely fended him off without either confirming or denying his hints. He reminded her at the end of the dance to come to his office on Monday.

"Sorry about that," Corrie apologized when she joined Bryan again. "Next dance I'll try to find you a more interesting partner."

Bryan put his arm around her waist and smiled mischievously. "I already have the most interesting partner in the room. If that's a polite way of saying you want to dance with the ex, you're going to have to fight me on the issue."

Dancing with Harry was the last thing she wanted. "But his wife is beautiful!" she pointed out.

"As I said, I've got the partner I want."

A thrill of pleasure rippled up her spine. They only parted for two other dances, both with older couples. Corrie noticed that Harry kept looking at them. She knew he wanted to change partners and dreaded the moment he made his move. To refuse would look gauche, but to accept would be worse. She no longer had anything to say to Harry. His lack of interest in his wife's flirting showed he didn't care about her and Corrie got the awful idea he might even try to resuscitate their old romance.

It finally happened. The music stopped, and Harry and Rhonda began walking toward them. They stopped and Harry said, "Corrie, one for old time's sake?"

"I—" She looked a question at Bryan.

"You've left it too late," Bryan said blandly. "We were just leaving. Sorry."

Corrie felt a great relief. "Sorry," she said with a smile.

Bryan took her firmly by the elbow and walked her out the door. He got her coat and helped her on with it, all without mentioning Harry. It wasn't until they were at the car that he turned to her.

"Well? Go on, tell me I didn't have any business answering your questions for you."

"I'm too grateful to be outraged." She laughed. "I was dreading that he'd ask me."

"I thought you loved him!"

"I thought so, too, once. I must have been crazy!"

"Corrie, you don't go to so much trouble to make a guy jealous if you don't still care for him a little."

"That was ages ago," she said, shaking her head at how foolish she'd been.

"Before Larry, you mean?" He peered down at her in the darkness. She looked uncertain, perplexed.

"You ask too many questions," she said and took the key to open the door herself and get inside.

She unlocked Bryan's door and handed him the keys when he got in. "It's not late," he said. "Want to go somewhere for a drink?"

"Do you want to?"

What Bryan wanted was to take her to bed, but as that required some explaining first, he said, "I could use a drink. It's been quite a night."

She laughed in pleasure that their night wasn't over yet. "You're not used to doing the fox-trot with ma-trons."

Bryan heard the anticipation in that laugh and gazed at her. "Wrong, Dear Corrie. I'm not used to seeing my date leer at another man. Now we're going to get some answers to those questions you've been avoiding all evening."

Chapter Eleven

Bryan didn't ask where she'd like to go or suggest they go to either her place or his. She was relieved not to have to make that decision. He drove past Mountainview to the Old Mill. The parking lot was crowded late on a Saturday night, but the maître d' found them a tiny table, about the size of a lamp stand. It was in a dark, private corner this time, away from the fire. The flickering candle in a handmade metal holder provided most of the illumination.

"White wine?" he asked.

"A peach schnapps and orange juice for me. The combination turns all bubbly and fuzzy. I'm becoming an addict."

When the maître d' left, Bryan gazed at her over the candle on their table. The wavering light played on her smiling face. Her expression was softly beaming, just the way he had so often pictured it.

"It's not a crease, definitely a dimple." His voice was unsteady as he reached across the table and touched her cheek gently.

The candlelight reflecting in his eyes gave a strange illusion of love light. Corrie felt shaken by that look. "It must be a shadow," she said.

"Since you won't let me compliment you, we'll agree to pretend it's a shadow." His hand fell from her cheek to rest on her arm. He moved his chair around closer to hers. Corrie noticed that Bryan had his back to the room.

"You can't see anything but the wall from that side! That was thoughtless of me."

His fingers tightened tentatively on her wrist. "I could see what I wanted to see perfectly. I just wanted to be able to reach you without getting burned by the candle." He lifted her hand, turned it and kissed the palm. The tender gesture left her shaken. That wasn't the act of a playboy. His eyes looked steadily into hers.

"Am I reaching you, Dear Corrie?" The seductive purr in his throat caused considerable damage to her heart. It felt like butter left too long in the sun.

There was a lambent glow in his eyes, and there was a promise in his smile. Oh Lord, he's going to seduce me! Corrie felt her composure scatter like autumn leaves.

She swallowed nervously and said, "What—" It came out in a squeak. She cleared her throat and tried again. "What made you change your mind?" It occurred to her that this vague question might require some explanation. He couldn't know she meant why was he coming on to her now, when he hadn't before. Bryan didn't ask her to explain.

"You." The word was a caress.

"Oh. What did I do?"

An impish grin broke. "You seduced me, you wanton woman. Seduced me with your New England morals and propriety and sexy red dress and dimple."

"Under the red dress and dimple, there beats the heart of a Pilgrim, Bryan," she warned sadly. It was true. Much as she wanted him to make mad, passionate love to her, she knew her upbringing would never allow it, any more than it had allowed her to give Harry a test run.

"Was Harry Danton a fellow Pilgrim?" he taunted.

"No, he wasn't. That's why we broke up."

"You mean..." A puzzled frown creased his brow.

"No hormonal workouts."

The frown eased to infinite satisfaction, only to return. "About Larry... You didn't answer my question."

Larry! She latched onto him like a lifeline. Bryan wouldn't try to take advantage of one of his own employees. Stealing an employee's girlfriend would be catastrophic for office morale.

"Larry feels as I do," she said primly.

The drinks arrived and Corrie picked hers up, eager to change the subject. "See how fizzy it is," she said inanely.

Bryan didn't even glance at her glass, but stared at her fixedly. "Georgie said you weren't seeing anyone special. If I'd known you were serious about him, I wouldn't have sent—"

He stopped and gave a guilty start. Corrie gave a little gasp as the truth dawned on her. He had sent Larry away on purpose! Anger began to roil inside her and inevitably found an outlet.

"You did it on purpose! You sent him away so you could take me to the party! I think you're disgusting, using your influence and power to—to sabotage one of your own employees."

"Darn it, Corrie, I wouldn't have done it if I'd known. When I asked Georgie to invite you to lunch she was supposed to find out just how things stood between you and Larry. I didn't think it could have gone very far yet. She told me you assured her it wasn't serious. He cut me out! Why shouldn't I try to cut myself back in? All's fair in love and war."

"What's love—if you'll pardon the expression—got to do with it?" Her voice sounded breathless and young, like Georgie's.

"Everything! Do you think I went to this much trouble just to have an affair? Asking Fred Helmer to have you do an article on Georgie, asking Georgie to make a special trip home from New York to ask you to lunch. I personally supervised the cutting of that T-bone, and you left half of it on your plate. I'm sorry about the salad dressing—and you didn't even try the chocolate cake!"

"But you looked ready to choke Georgie when she asked me to stay."

"I was ready to throttle her for adding herself to the party. She was supposed to dart off as soon as I arrived. She got everything mixed up. You were still supposed to be at the table. It's your fault. You were supposed to try the chocolate cake.''

Corrie just stared, speechless. In her mind she saw Theo in an apron, worrying about the whipped cream and spaghetti sauce. She remembered the little blue velvet box. I'm going to pop the question, he had said.

"I know how you feel about life, Corrie. I've been reading your articles since the first night I met you. Why do you think I've been trying to hold myself back? Swearing I wouldn't call you, then finding an excuse to visit the *Herald* offices. I had to at least see you. Running out of my office when I knew you were coming, then flying back, hoping you hadn't left yet.''

"But you didn't act as if you liked me,'' she pointed out.

"If I acted like a frightened hare, it's because I liked you too much. I was forcing myself not to touch you, to see you again until I was sure. Now I'm sure.''

She gave him an incredulous look. "Of what?'' Her voice was a whisper.

"That I love you.''

"I don't think you know anything about love, Bryan. It's more than just sex.''

"I don't know firsthand about kids and hamburgers, but I'm willing to learn. I want to marry you, Corrie. If you and Larry have already come to terms, naturally I...''

He saw the peculiar way she stared at him. "Kids? Hamburgers?'' she asked in confusion.

"Like the couple in the restaurant. I want kids and hamburgers.''

"But you made that sneering remark about the joys of parenthood!"

"It wasn't sneering. Pitying, maybe. I listen to the married guys at work talking about their mortgages and their kids. I used to pity them. Now I realize it was me I was pitying, or maybe despising for being too big a coward to tackle it myself. You hit the nail on the head. 'You want a challenge—you're looking at it,' you said. Raising a family is the last great challenge. Having a wife like you is the reward. Lord, I sound maudlin!" he said and looked surprised at what had come pouring out of his mouth.

"No!" she said quickly. "No, not maudlin. Just a little sentimental."

Bryan moved his chair until it touched hers. He put one arm over the back of her chair, his hand touching her hair, his fingers brushing the nape of her neck. "You've already answered the question about Harry and the hormones—not that I have any right to ask. I haven't been a saint myself. The Larry thing is more serious. Do you love him?"

She slowly turned her head and met his gaze. He saw the laughter lurking in the depths of her eyes.

"I've got five strong fingers poised to tighten around your neck if you say the wrong thing," he warned her. His smile softened the words to a love charm. The fingers stroked her nape lovingly, sending shivers down her spine.

Corrie felt tears boiling behind her eyes. Was she crazy, crying at the happiest moment of her life? "And if I say the right thing, what do those five strong fingers do?" she asked.

"Say you love me and I'll show you."

She gazed at him long and hard. "I think I could learn to love you."

His fingers tightened. "I hope for your sake that you're a real fast learner, Dear Corrie. I have only minimal control over these digits."

She reached up and took his fingers lightly in hers. "That's all right. I can control them. Can I have another drink? It's delicious. We'll raise your digits and signal the waiter." She lifted his arm.

The waiter came. "Check, please," Bryan said. He put a bill on the table and pulled back Corrie's chair.

They went hand-in-hand to the parking lot. A hint of winter was in the air that night. The wind was cold. It pulled at her coat and blew up her back, but she didn't mind. She gave a little shiver and hurried into the car.

When Bryan got in, his expression was serious, almost brooding. Corrie felt a wave of apprehension that he was already regretting his outburst of sentiment. He moved closer to her and put his arm around her shoulders. As soon as he spoke, she knew he hadn't changed his mind. His voice was still warm.

"I don't know where to begin," he said simply. "I got off on such a terrible footing with you from the start, loudly proclaiming my aversion to marriage. I thought you were... I don't know. It sounded as though you and Theo had been cruising the world together."

"That was Theo's fault, maybe partly my fault, too," she added thoughtfully.

"I admit, at the beginning, I only wanted to have an affair with you. That lasted until our first visit to this place, when you went and turned into my kid sister. And you know how I protect my kid sister from lechers—like me."

"But you asked me out after that."

"A long time after," he reminded her. "I'd been such an angel I decided I deserved a reward. Just a friendly afternoon with you. Then you did it again. You went and changed from Georgie into the woman I wanted to marry, except that I didn't want to be married."

"I could see the kids put you off at that old inn," she said thoughtfully.

"No, Corrie, I put myself off with my selfishness. I thought about those kids a lot that week. That little girl. I wished she was mine—ours," he amended. "And by the time I'd made up my mind to ask you to marry me, you went and changed again. You were suddenly Larry's girlfriend, with the added complication that Larry happens to be my employee. In a fit of jealousy I handed my date with you over to him and even pretended I had to go to New York this weekend."

"Then you sent Larry away," she charged.

"First I promoted him, to make it possible."

"Bryan! That's—that's immoral! A misuse of power."

"As I said, all's fair in love and war. And I didn't do it until you told Georgie you didn't care for him. Now comes the big question," he said and drew a long, worried breath. "Do you think you could love me enough to marry me? With time, I mean, after a proper courtship.''

She gazed at his face, shadowed in the moonlight that beamed through the car window. Every fiber of her body loved him. She lifted her fingers to trace the planes of his jaw and cheeks. Her voice was fogged with love. ''It's funny. I advise other people to give an ultimatum when they find a noncommittal-type person. I never even had a chance to give you an ultimatum. I broke all my own rules. My mind refused to forget you....''

''Corrie! Dear Corrie,'' he moaned and touched his lips to her eyes. He felt the tang of salt from an unshed tear. Love swelled inside him until it seemed too big for his body to contain. He wanted to love and cherish this woman, to possess and protect her, but without changing her independence. She was perfect just as she was.

''And I knew I'd never forget you,'' he murmured. His lips began sliding down her cheek in a hot caress.

A tremor shook her body and she pressed close to make sure he was real. She lifted her arms and locked them behind his neck so she could see him and still be close. She moved invitingly against him, stirring him to a nearly uncontrollable desire.

His voice was husky with it, ragged and rough. ''I've been wanting to do this ever since—'' She stopped him by placing her lips on his and kissed him to silence. He crushed her in his arms until she was molded to his body, which seemed to have been custom designed for hers, and still it wasn't close enough.

He scooped her onto his lap without breaking the embrace. Love flared to passion as one kiss burned into the next in a frenzied fever that left her breathless. When she stopped a moment to collect her senses, she leaned her head against his shoulder.

"It seems we won't have to worry about body chemistry anyway," she said in a small voice.

"That's my department. I am a chemist after all," he said, trying for a light touch. His body quivered with the effort of restraining his passion.

His hands moved gently over her body, which was soft and relaxed against him. His fingers twitched as he palmed one breast in his hand. He wanted to feel it without the dress, to feel the silky texture of her flesh on his. His hand moved down, taking the measure of her feminine hips, down over her thighs, expecting every instant that she'd object.

He smiled in the darkness, perfectly satisfied, when Corrie placed her hand over his and drew it gently but firmly to her lap. "We'll have to go home tomorrow for you to meet my mom and dad," she said.

His throaty chuckle echoed in her ear. "Good psychology, my love, but I didn't intend to do anything your parents wouldn't like. I've waited all my life for someone like you. I can wait a little longer."

"Only a little longer." She sighed happily. Some things were worth waiting for. Love, and Bryan Holmes, were definitely two of them.

* * * * *

Silhouette Romance™

Legendary Lovers Trilogy

BY DEBBIE MACOMBER....

ONCE UPON A TIME, in a land not so far away, there lived a girl, Debbie Macomber, who grew up dreaming of castles, white knights and princes on fiery steeds. Her family was an ordinary one with a mother and father and one wicked brother, who sold copies of her diary to all the boys in her junior high class.

One day, when Debbie was only nineteen, a handsome electrician drove by in a shiny black convertible. Now Debbie knew a prince when she saw one, and before long they lived in a two-bedroom cottage surrounded by a white picket fence.

As often happens when a damsel fair meets her prince charming, children followed, and soon the two-bedroom cottage became a four-bedroom castle. The kingdom flourished and prospered, and between soccer games and car pools, ballet classes and clarinet lessons, Debbie thought about love and enchantment and the magic of romance.

One day Debbie said, "What this country needs is a good fairy tale." She remembered how well her diary had sold and she dreamed again of castles, white knights and princes on fiery steeds. And so the stories of Cinderella, Beauty and the Beast, and Snow White were reborn....

Look for Debbie Macomber's *Legendary Lovers* trilogy from Silhouette Romance: *Cindy and the Prince* (January, 1988); *Some Kind of Wonderful* (March, 1988); *Almost Paradise* (May, 1988). Don't miss them!

SRT-1

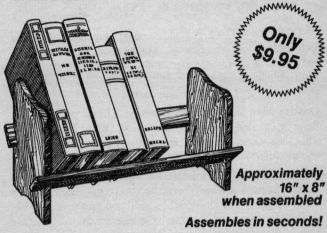

COMING NEXT MONTH

#550 A MATTER OF HONOR—Brittany Young
FBI agent Tori Burton always got her man—but now the man she really wanted
was Adam Danaro. Adam had agreed to help Tori with her latest case, but his
family had always been on the wrong side of the law. Could Tori trust him with
her life...and her heart?

#551 THE BEWITCHING HOUR—Jennifer Mikels
T.J. Hawkins had left Samantha Tyler years ago to become a football star. Now
that he was back, Samantha was determined not to get hurt again. But T.J. had
learned from his mistakes—he knew he had to prove to Samantha that the time
for their love had finally come...

#552 HOUSE CALLS—Terry Essig
Andrea Conrades was not about to let Gregory Rennolds, M.D., railroad her
into marriage—even if he could prove the chemistry between them with one
devastating kiss....

#553 SEASON OF THE HEART—Pat Warren
When journalist Laura Franklin decided to get the scoop on a new Colorado ski
lodge, she'd expected an icy reception from its media-hating owner, former
Olympic medalist Dan Kramer. She never guessed Dan would warm to her. If
she returned his feelings, would she be skating on thin ice?

#554 AUTHOR'S CHOICE—Elizabeth August
If Melinda Oliver wanted to keep the custody of her niece and nephew she'd
have to find a temporary husband—fast! Handsome adventure writer
John Medwin was willing, but what would he do when he discovered Melinda
had concocted a story of her own—a romance between the two of them?

#555 CINDY AND THE PRINCE—Debbie Macomber
(Book One of the LEGENDARY LOVERS Trilogy)
Cindy Territo believed in fairy tales—in one night she'd convinced hard-headed
executive Thorndike Prince that she was his real-life Cinderella. Cindy was in
love, but how was she going to keep her prince from discovering that she was
also the person who cleaned his office?

AVAILABLE THIS MONTH: